OLD BILL

DAVE KINCAID

- WRITER OF LOVE -

WESTBOW
PRESS®
A DIVISION OF THOMAS NELSON
& ZONDERVAN

WestBow Press books may be ordered through booksellers or by contacting:

WestBow Press
A Division of Thomas Nelson & Zondervan
1663 Liberty Drive
Bloomington, IN 47403
www.westbowpress.com
1 (866) 928-1240

ISBN: 978-1-4497-0332-5 (sc)
ISBN: 978-1-4497-0334-9 (hc)
ISBN: 978-1-4497-0333-2 (e)

Library of Congress Control Number: 2010931007

Print information available on the last page.

WestBow Press rev. date: 02/24/2017

DEDICATION

I wish to dedicate this writing to the Lord first. It is my hope that he can use it to His glory, honor and service.

My thanks goes to Bill and Grace Bush who had the perseverance, through faith in God, to stay married for those many decades. Because they stayed together, I was able to have a piece of a family, by their example, they set the standard for a husband and wife. Their enduring relationship should be emulated and revered.

God Bless them and you always.

Dave Kincaid, Author

CONTENTS

PREFORWARD

*H*ello! From the Author of "Old Bill", Dave Kincaid. This is my first book. This book and one dollar will get you a coffee at McDonalds or six dollars plus, if you are at Starbucks Wow!

I have always had the desire to write. One time when I was in public high school I was given an assignment in literature class. I wrote out the story but was told that I couldn't write on a subject that was religious or had religious thoughts in it.

The teacher even had my mother come up to school to talk with her about my work.

It is wonderful to live in a free country but it is so sad that God is being intentionally left out of our schools and society.

What the system did to me that day was stop me from writing until now, as a grown up.

What the public system has done to itself is replace the Ten Commandments with metal detectors at the door.

On a page of this book you will find a conversation between a teacher, Mrs. Roberts and some students. You will notice or be reminded how America has lost her innocence.

This is a "Christian" book. My second book, will be the same, Christian based.

Please, if you will, excuse the spelling, grammar and any other technical problems that you notice.

The main characters, Bill and Grace Bush are real people in my life.

You truly can do all things through God who will strengthen you. I do hope you enjoy the book and it blesses you.

May God Bless you and yours always.

Dave Kincaid

FORWARD

———•—•———

I don't presume to be a writer. Considering I'm a sheet metal worker by trade.

I have never written anything before. My inspiration comes from fond memories of my relatives. It does seem that to often the deceased pass to quickly from our memory.

I know you can't brood or bring them back, sadly though, death seems so final.

This is why being a Christian believer gives such security. Death isn't final unless it is the second death. Most people don't know about that, or there would be a mad rush to get saved next Sunday.

We all live forever; we need to make a choice where we are going to go for an eternity.

Death is, not going to paradise.

I'm curtain that between Microsoft word and spell check and my Oldest Grandson,

Mitchell, who can spell very well, I will write a book. I'm taking a chance but in life you only go around once. Mitch also did the artwork you see in this book.

I have a disclaimer. The sacrifice that Uncle Bill made going to War in Europe isn't to be belittled by the fiction part of this story.

Bill nearly died from pneumonia after lying in cold, muddy trenches for days. He also had a collapsed lung as well.

I have worked every winter, part time on this book for some years. I hope it has something for you.

I have some faith in this writing. I want it to be a success and a movie for all to see.

Matthew17:20 - He replied, because you have so little faith. I tell you the truth, if you have faith as small as a mustard seed, you can say to this mountain, move from here to there and it will move. Nothing will be impossible for you.

*Definition of the word imagination / the power to form mental images. Please use yours.

LIST OF CHARACTERS

Bills family
Bills father (Poppa)
Bills mother (Momma)
Bills brother#1 - Oland
Bills brother#2 - Grelton
Bills brother #3 - Alton
Bills brother#4 - Erie
Bills only sister - Suzette
Bill, himself - William Casper Bush
Child hood and life long, friend - Dale Bird
Franklin Bird – Dale's brother
Dale Birds - Mother
Dales Birds - Father
Mrs. Roberts the school teacher for all the young people
Church friends
Childhood and lifelong friend - Moses Johnson
Otis Johnson - brother to Moses
Otto the old German pilot
Rudy - Great-Great Grandson to Otto
Hanna - Otto's deceased wife
British soldier

Salesman at the book store

Jonah, Grandson of the older man in Nineveh

Grace - Bills wife

Old man in the town of Nineveh

Bills army drill instructor Jessie Stales

Hazel - Graces sister

Rebecca - Dale Birds woman friend

Maybelle Johnson - Bills nurse at Fort Funston

PREFACE

————•——•————

*G*reat Uncle Bill Bush has been gone now for some years and is still missed by all of us. Just bragging about his long life gave us hope for a long physical life ourselves.

Not everyone can make it to the century mark or more in years old, but Bill did. He made it to 103. I'm back visiting his grave site. I took the time because I was close by. I was on the way to look at some work in Brookfield, Missouri. I made a rubbing of the inscriptions on the head stones. It reads "Wm. C. Bush and Grace" Grace made her home going 10 years before Bill did.

I would think by now you are asking yourself, who these two decreased people are and who is doing this writing? I can tell you that I'm very sentimental and those two people loved each other and I loved them both. Bill and Grace were together 65years, and were separated temporally by death. They would be every married couple's heroes. They are the type of people you see in one of those oval shaped frames. Their families have saved them because it is a classic picture that captures two young people some ninety years ago. The people in the picture are long since gone but their lives make a great story.

Like most books or stories you need a title. I've had quite a time deciding on a title for this book. I've had many ideas to choose from. "The oval picture', "a button and a knife", or "the carving" all of these need explaining. I prefer the simple but more appropriate title of "OLD BILL".

To give some back ground here my sisters, whom are twins to each other but not identical twins and myself would go visit Bill and Grace in the fifty's, when we were growing up. We drove up from Kansas City, Kansas in a 1955, light, green, four, door, Ford Galaxy. We didn't have seat belts to use. My dad saved our lives one day avoiding a driver in our lane passing on a hill. Dad swerved far right on the shoulder to avoid the oncoming car, what an experience as I was leaning up on the front seat behind Mom.

I personally remember Grace as if were yesterday. She was taller than Bill he was only 5 ft. 8 inches. Grace always had on an apron. It was one of those aprons with the frilly stuff on the shoulders.

Uncle Bill always had on blue, bib overalls. Bill was either tending to the garden or the beehives one of his other past times was whittling. Considering Bill had beehives we were never without honey when we were there. Fresh honeycomb, honey to go on Graces fresh made biscuits you can't beat that combination. It makes you wish time would stand still. Simple things like honeycomb honey, fresh garden grown tomatoes, cold watermelon, and don't forget the corn on the cob make life good.

I guess most of Bill and Graces young life had been lived by the time my sisters and I met them. I was one of those baby boomers, a war baby born after WW2, in June of 1949. I was spoiled and removed from reality by the way of the invention of the television set. Bill and grace were not removed from reality they were real down to earth, God believing, Christian people.

Elva Grace Whitacre and William Casper Bush were married April 26, 1925 in Chillicothe, Missouri. I have a copy of the marriage certificate. Bill and Grace wanted children but lost three due to miscarriage before Donna Fern was born to them on July3, 1934.

Bill and Grace lived in a red brick house on the East side of Chillicothe. This is where my sisters, Terrie and Kerrie and I would visit. I wish to share some family genealogy. Grace is my Great Aunt or sister to my Grandmother Hazel. Hazel and Grace whenever these two sisters were together they were always laughing, like two little kids. They were in their own world with their own language seemingly with no cares to worry about at all. This is a testimony to their togetherness and love for each other.

I'm going to rely on Aunt Betty to have some stories about these two sisters. Betty is Hazel's oldest daughter. Hazel had two daughters and two sons.

One of her boys is my father, Stanley was his name and the other is my direct Uncle. Bill is his name. Bill and Stan both joined the Navy during World War two. Bill was on a destroyer and shot at some of those kamikaze diver bombers. Dad was a Seabee they built the airplane landing strips out of jungle in the Pacific. Hazels other daughter was named Marilyn she died young leaving behind five children. Betty became their fill in mom. Betty did a great job too.

If fact Betty needs even more credit for taking care of her mom and dad, Hazel and Grandpa Walter When they were older. They would eventually pass away at her home in Kansas City, Kansas. Thank-you, Betty. This is a good example of how to take care of older parents, just like they did for us. Betty's dad my grandfather was named Walter and I have his name as a middle name. Every other Saturday night my father would take me to Grandpa Walters's house in Kansas City, Kansas to have Grandpa cut my hair. We would go down into the basement next to the largest gravity furnace known to man. Then we walked back further to a corner where the hair cut would happen under a single, hanging light, you know the kind of light that was a light bulb that swings back and forth after you pull the metal chain. I would get more of a buzz with some hair left on top for a haircut. While this haircut was going on, my father, Stanley and Grandpa Walter would talk shop and about worldly things but never to me. I truly loved them both despite them ignoring me.

This gives you some background and knowledge of our family and whom Bill is related to, just some common mid-west people.

It is my belief though, that Midwest people are in reality much more than common. So many have been much more. A short list of some would include General John J. Pershing coming from just down the road from Chillicothe in Laclede Missouri. General Dwight D Eisenhower of Abilene Kansas, Amelia Earhart of Atchison, Kansas. Later on you have men like Harry Truman of Independence Missouri. Walt Disney, Chicago, Illinois. Walt formally lived and started in Kansas City, Missouri.

THE WOUNDS

The wounds go deep they stay concealed,
The wounds don't heal they bleed and bleed,
The wounds are all without answers God has those,
The wounds are fresh as today but are old and dusty,
The wounds are now part of our characters,
The wounds give out pain we all share it,
The wounds are many scars that have formed,
The wounds go deeper and deeper,
The wounds are a burden too heavy to bear alone,
The wounds are there but so is God,
The wounds of the past are given to God if you are man enough,
The wounds are there but God is healing now,
The wounds and God build our character,
The wounds are now accepted and we are more the man,
Praise God for the wound so we can be a Christian man.

Dave Kincaid, Author

JUST A WHILE AGO

———•••———

Not that long ago you were a squirming, crying baby, going gently to sleep on my chest.

Just a moment ago you started to walk and chew on the furniture, like a puppy dog.

It wasn't that long ago you started to talk and renamed our dog.

It couldn't have been that long ago you got cut by your eye and I felt your pain as you were stitched up.

It really wasn't that long ago you came in and flipped on that light switch that was always out of your reach.

Not long ago we enjoyed the circus and the go cart.

Much too long ago now you said "I LOVE YOU" as you must have said one million times before.

Just a while ago I remembered these things and I said "I LOVE YOU FOR ALWAYS."

Dave Kincaid, Author

AMAZING GRACE

———————

*G*race wasn't always old, just like Bill wasn't always old. I just had never seen them any other way in my lifetime. After all these years I found out that Grace isn't her first name, her given name was Elva Grace Whitacre. She was born in 1903. This made her 9 years younger than Bill. This would have made her fourteen years old when WW1 started, nineteen or twenty when Bill was back recovering at Fort Funston (modern day, now Fort Riley in Kansas) She is 23 years old when she is married to Bill.

Grace what a beautiful name for a beautiful person. That name fit precisely her personality, always smiling and happy and encouraging to others. Grace was a generous, unselfish, hardworking woman. Grace's secret was that she had a joyful heart with the Lord. *Proverbs 15:30* A cheerful look brings joy to the heart and good news health to the bones. Read *I Thessalonians 5:16-18* Be joyful always; pray continually, give thanks in all circumstances for this is God's will for you in Jesus Christ.

Philippians 4:4-5 "Rejoice in the Lord always. Let your gentleness be evident to all."

Grace was a fine figure of a woman too; she was tall, of slim build, with curly brown hair and blue eyes.

Grace should have been a nurse she was a very caring person. She took care of different people in the neighborhood when they were sick. She would take flowers to them and meals if needed especially the elderly. Grace could cook anything too, especially pies, pies of all kinds she was known for how delicious they were.

During World War One, Grace took a job as a candy maker for Brown and Bird Candy Company in Chillicothe, Missouri. She was in demand as a chocolate "dipper". There was quite a "knack" to making hand dipped chocolate covered candies. She would sit in a cool basement area working at an electric table that kept the chocolate at just the right temperature for "dipping" If the chocolate was to warm it could "run". Too cool and it could get milky white.

When Grace was younger and still at home she and her sister Hazel and their brother Orville lost their dad to a fire. The fire was in the family garden. No one was able to explain how the accident happened. It was a horrible tragedy. Their Father, Henry was burning off the family garden, this was in November, getting ready for next year's planting. Somehow, Henry had caught his clothes on fire, he panicked and inhaled smoke. Before anyone could help, Henry was gone.

Grace and Hazel are walking calmly home giggling together that day when HAZEL!!!! GRACE!!! A franc, neighbor is yelling out YOUR PA!!, YOUR PA!!, COME QUICKLY!!!. When the girls arrived in the back yard their father was on the ground. There was nothing the girls could do. The two sisters are wearing full length winter coats, they fall to their knees holding each other as they cry, and the tears don't stop for some time. The neighbor, Mrs. Pike holds them both for more time and finally says, "Let's pray".

Mrs. Pike prays "The Lord is my shepherd. I shall not want. He makes me to lie down in green pastures He leads me beside quiet waters, he restores my soul, He guides me in paths of righteousness for his name's sake. Even though I walk through the valley of death,

I will fear no evil, for you are with me, your rod and staff, they comfort me.

You prepare a table before me in the presence of my enemies. You anoint my head with oil my cup overflows. Surely goodness and love will follow me all the days of my life, and I will dwell in the house of the Lord forever. This is the *23rd Psalm* used for the prayer.

"Hold me" Grace, Hazel says, "hold me, hold me, hold me, hold me as she and her sister cry more tears of sorrow and grief". Orville came in from some farm work he had only to find his Father on the table being cleaned by his beloved sisters. The pain and shock of seeing his father's dead body was horrifying for him. Orville's knees buckle, after some time, Orville cry's out in pain AHHH!!! And hits his fists on the floor, Orville with his head down gains enough strength to ask, what happened?

It was a long night of no sleep that night as the siblings reminisce about old times together as a family doing things with their Father and Mother. Having fun times just being together as a family and with their church family and church activities.

They even had worked with their father in that same garden for many years to have fresh vegetables and to allow much canning for the winter months that always came.

As they lay on the front room floor that night Orville says, Hazel do you remember that big catfish we caught together? Father had to help us bring it in it was so big and we were little. "Yes" "I remember a great day of fishing". We all caught plenty that day.

"Yes" and we had to clean them too, speaks up Grace. Many stories were shared that night.

Unfortunately that next day the sisters and brother have the responsibility of making the arrangements for their Fathers burial through their church and the Pastor.

Orville makes his own Father's casket in their shared wood shop. Orville is in the shop building, carefully surveying the wood supply he selects some three quarter thick, red oak that will need planed out. Working that night until he is nearly asleep Orville is back early the next morning with sore arms to finish sanding and give a clear coat finish over the red oak, casket. Orville finishes the lid with a plain wood cross. The casket is of good craftsmanship a trait handed down from his Father to son.

Pastor Greg delivers a wonderful eulogy for Henry Whitacre. Henry was a good, Christian, Father, obedient to God's law. This will be what he is remembered for, keeping the law. He has now gone to be with the Lord while preparing the garden for planting next year's vegetables. Henry now rests with the Lord.

We never know when we will go to be with the Lord. This is something we need not know only God knows. It is best that way, it is God's plan. We can't live a life of fear but a life of anticipation for the coming savior. Everyone in Chillicothe, Missouri was at Henry's wake and subsequent funeral. There was a long elegy by Pastor Greg. He was remembering good times for the family and Henry's devotion to his Church. This same pastor had married Henry and Rose some thirty years before. Rose has been ten years bed ridden from a problem no one knows what it is.

All the family grieved like Christian's grieve with hope. This hope is that Henry went straight to heaven. Titus1: 2, Romans 8:24 & 25, John 3:15 and 16. That everyone who believes in Jesus may have eternal life. ""For God so loved the world that he gave his one and only son, that whoever believes in him shall not perish but have eternal life".

The Holy Bible scriptures tell us there is hope and eternal life for the believer. Orville did take the death very hard. The loss of a good, father at his young age was tuff. Orville would eventually, grow up to be a Christian Pastor.

Grace and Hazel grew closer over the next few years and stayed that way the rest of their long, life's, relying on each other.

They would go their separate ways only when they were married. Hazel would be married to Walter Kincaid and eventually moved to Kansas City where Walter worked as a meat deliveryman for the Wilson Meat Packing Company.

Over all, life in Chillicothe was simple and slow for Grace and her siblings. There still was plenty of life and fun to be had, being a Christian isn't boring.

When the 1st World War began there was more excitement and anxiety because of the young men that were willingly, signing up to go and fight. Chillicothe was a main train station for all of the surrounding towns including Breckenridge where Bill Bush and his family lived. As the different trains would leave with some of the boys going to boot camp. Grace and some of the youth group at church would take cookies and milk to them as they boarded. The cookies were a nice "send-off" for the boys, some of whom didn't make it back. Grace didn't notice much of the one young boy going off to War from Breckenridge, Bill Bush. He would become her life mate.

When Bill did get back from the World War 1 he was more active in church. He joined the same church that Grace went to. It just so happened that one of the first activities at the church was an all- church picnic. Grace was there wearing a white, frilly, summer dress and hat. Grace has grown up these last few years. She was serving up cold drinks on a hot summer's day.

"Hello" Bill said to her with that 'Texas drawl' speech he had (no one knows where the "drawl" came from) and that "hello", was all it took for her he was wearing his Army uniform at the time, looking so handsome. The two of them fell in love over the next few weeks and by December, Bill proposed Marriage to her. The now couple were engaged to be married that next April. They would always be chaperoned during their engagement,

Hazel, her sister was with them. Hazel was also one of Grace's bride's maids at her wedding. The wedding was nice with many church friends present.

Bill along with his brother and friends built a red brick house for Grace. The story was that the basement was hand dug out by Bill and his brother. Bill and Grace would live there for many decades.

Grace was a good and Godly wife for Bill; she is a true jewel a rare find.

Proverbs 31:10 through 31 tells of the virtuous wife. A wife of noble character who can find? She is worth far more than rubies These Proverbs verses go on and on how well she takes care of her household.

Likewise, Bill was a good and devoted husband to her. He worked hard and provided well. *Ephesians 5:25* "Husbands love your wives, just as Christ loved the church and gave himself up for her."

Bill and Grace together were good parents raising their only child, Donna, in the church. Chillicothe would be the place where Grace would spend the majority of her long, life. Later in life when Grace was about 80 years old she had to have a pace- maker installed for her heart. Her heart wanted to skip a beat or two. She was fine with the pacemaker and did well with it. She even had new batteries installed at different times; Grace would even joke about it. Saying she was really "charged up now".

Grace would become a second Grandmother to my sisters and me. Even though those visits stopped because of family troubles, I loved her just as though she was my own Grandmother and so did my sisters.

BILL GROWING UP

Uncle Bill's draft registration card.

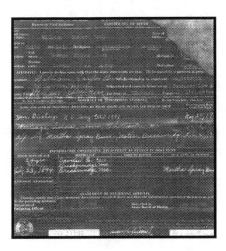

Bill's delayed Birth certificate showing July 25th 1894 for his birth date.

*T*he date is July 26th 1908 we are close to Breckenridge, in North Central Missouri. Breckenridge is "broken ridge" in the German language. We are at the rural farmhouse of the Bush family. Just for the record the Bush family is of German heritage coming out to the plains as settlers back in 1872.

The evening is not just hot but it is more a sultry, humid, summer evening, it is one of those screen door slamming nights with little breeze. Air conditioning was a luxury not heard of yet. Nor is there indoor plumbing or electricity. Dinner is over the dishes are done but Momma is still working in the kitchen. It is that time of the evening that everyone in the Bush family has been waiting for" the evening checker games. The boys are anxious to get started and are already in a tiff. "Hurry Poppa", the boys have the board ready and have started the first game, Bill is frustrated, Alton is too young to play, he doesn't understand the game, and Erie and Poppa enter the kitchen. Momma would stop her work finally and remove her wet and soiled, apron. She still had to tend to baby, Suzette the only daughter in the family.

No! Alton, you can't go backwards! Poppa he is going backwards. Make him stop. Now, now boys Alton needs to learn just like you did when you were little. Papa says okay, Alton let me in there, now, who is first tonight? I'm ready for you Poppa proclaims Bill, the oldest son. This is the moment all have been waiting for the entire room falls dead silent. Everyone takes the game very seriously as each and every move is meticulously thought out. Each boy gets a turn with Poppa at the checkerboard. Time seams to fly by and two hours are gone faster than a jackrabbit across the front yard. Poppa would take no prisoners while playing the game, all of this checker playing made Bill and his brothers' great players.

Time to stop and go to bed Papa says. All you hear is the "AAH" of disappointment. Now after the boys are ready for bed it is time for the nightly devotions. "I'm reading tonight" Bill offers to read, yes Bill, thank-you says Papa. This is a how everyday ends with the nightly Bible, devotions. Everyone treasures the devotions. Devotions make the difference in there day to day lives. These are the instructions from God. Instructions on how to live with each other, and how to love one another. Momma and Papa pray with each child as they go to sleep. The Bible is a huge blessing when many questions like, where did the stars come from? And where did we come from, are asked. All of the 31 Proverbs Chapters come in handy, tonight is *Proverbs 27: 1-27* Bill reads "do not boast about tomorrow, for you do not know what a day may bring forth". Each child that can read reads a few other verses. Poppa says a prayer then the candle goes out for the night's sleep.

Everyone on the Bush farm works hard and plays even harder. Not everything is about work in Bill's life; next to the game of baseball and the checker games there is hunting and fishing of all kinds. In North Missouri wildlife is very plentiful. There is a long list a different animals to hunt we have white tail deer, mule deer, ring-neck pheasant, bobwhite quail, and there are lots of wet lands for water fowl like ducks and Canadian geese. There is a natural fly way for the migrating birds that stretches between Chillicothe and Breckenridge. Bill, his brother's and friends would hunt for all of these different animals, not necessarily in the order given but sometimes all in one day's time. The boys have deer stands in the woods and know the deer paths and deer habits.

One of the favorites to hunt is the ring-neck pheasant. This beautiful bird, was introduced to the American, prairie in the 1800's, they flourished in that tall, wavy prairie grass, let us listen to a morning hunt.

"Grelton"! Grelton! Are you going out today? Grelton wake up! It is nearly 4:30, get up! OK! Bill, Grelton says as he rolls out rubbing his eyes. I'm sorry Bill, help me find my boots, Thanks! That was quick. Come on!! We need to meet up with Dale says Bill. You get the dogs I will get the guns shells and water. "Yes Bill" Grelton says with respect to the older brother, Bill, is in charge of the hunt. The boys are going to meet up with Dale Bird from the next farm over to the West and then head out to the eighty-acre patch of prairie grass, where the pheasants roost. Two sides of the acreage is blocked out with hedge trees. This area is great cover for the birds, that's why they roost there. The boys each have one dog. Bill has a very good-looking tri colored English setter, named "Brutus". Grelton has a strong, chocolate colored, German short hair. Dale has a young, white female pointer with only a half season's experience. "Hi Dale" says Bill it looks as though we will be there by daybreak. "Yes" we will and Good morning to you both. Dale was always a happy personality. As the boys walk they make their plan of how to hunt that morning. You know what happened last time says Dale; yes they got out the back corner. We need to block them. Okay I will block, Dale says. Just give me enough time to get up there before you start into the field. The dogs are getting anxious and are pulling hard on their leashes. There is just enough predawn light to see the birds beautiful, plumage. The wind is blowing some and there is that late November, and fall, chill in the air and the boys can see their breath. As they wait for Dale to get set, the leaves are swirling and rustling, around their feet." Let's get going, let the dogs loose."

Pepper and Daisy start in with noses to the ground. They go only twenty yards when Daisy goes on point. Grelton yells out "POINT" then "COCK" then the first shots "boom -boom" and Bill has his first bird and yells out "dead" "Good dog" there is much excitement all at once with Pepper as the dog retrieves a large cock pheasant and brings it to the feet of Bill. Grelton what happened? Why didn't you shoot? I still had my "safety" on when the birds got up, you know how that is. In the distance you can hear more shots, boom, boom, boom, boom, the booms really echo through the early, morning. Dale is seeing birds too. Then more shots are heard. Finally when Bill and Grelton moved through the field and they find Dale. The hunters can hardly believe their eyes. Dale has shot three birds an almost unbelievable feat.

The boy's all become good marksman with the shotguns and the deer rifle. This skill will help Bill and Dale when they go off to war.

The boys know they are going to hunt that day after school so they take their deer rifles to school. "BUSH BOYS" Dale was included in the "Bush boys" like he was another one of the brothers, "PUT THOSE GUNS UP and GET IN YOUR SEATS QUICKLY" says Mrs. Roberts, the teacher. "Yes, Mrs. Roberts". Mrs. Roberts rules her class with a red dowel rod. If you speak out of turn you would get the rod across the knuckles. Once in a while someone would act up in class and get the red dowel right across the top of the knuckles, and that hurts! *Proverbs 13-24* He who spares the rod hates his son, but he who loves him disciplines him promptly.

Life for the boys is going well. Another good friend that Bill has is Moses Johnson and his brother Otis. They are from a black family that goes to the same church as the other boys. They like to play baseball after church. With these two black boys, Dale and his brother, Bill and his two brothers we have the core group of friends that play together.

The Bush family had lost a young son Bill's brother Alton to appendicitis.

These are good boys who have a tight bond together. They are best friends for life. *Proverbs 17:17.* A friend loves at all times and a brother is born for adversity. The tranquility of their lives seems not to be broken but life is not that way, a darker day is coming for them all and it starts with Dale's Mom, Mrs. Bird.

It was a beautiful spring day with an unexpected death of a young mother of two. The story of her death is a simple one. Mrs. Bird was found in her back yard, doing her day to day chores. About half a basket of clothes that she was hanging was still in the basket. She had died suddenly, totally unexpected found slumped over her basket of clothes. Mrs. Bird had gone to meet the Lord in her backyard. She was an irreplaceable and priceless wife. The bible says she is more precious than rubies *Proverbs 31:10* and is to be esteemed more than our own self. She is more valuable that gold.

There was a beautiful funeral but very emotional for all of the local children. For the close friends it was very hard and especially hard on Bill and his brothers. This one happening to Bill's best friend would affect him deeply and the whole community. Shortly after his wife's death Mr. Bird moved to Kansas City, Missouri, taking Dale and his brother with him. He was going to work on large construction project the new train station the Union Station.

This train station project was to start in 1911 and be completed by October 1914.

The completion would be just in time for the soldiers to use it going to war. Now, Bill has lost his best friend too. Neither Bill nor Dale had any idea they would meet just a few years later when they go off to war. Losing a friend is tuff. What is the value of a friend? *Proverbs 27:17* As iron sharpens iron so a man sharpens the countenance of his friend. There had been many happy days of play before all of this happens to the Bird family and the community.

As Bill grows up he has baseball to play and snow to play in. Just regular fun things that boys do while growing up. Baseball was America's game by 1900. The rules for the game were invented by Abner Doubleday one day in 1839. Baseball's song "take me out to the ball game" was wrote by Jack Norworth in 1908. Bill was born one year before the famous baseball player Babe Ruth who was born in 1895. We know today the Star Spangled Banner as the song always sung at ball games today but no one did that until the 1918 World Series because of the patriotic feelings about the war in

Europe. It would be another 14 years before the song would become the official National Anthem for America.

One afternoon, after the Sunday, services all the boys of the church started a baseball game. Now selecting the players for each team was a long standing tradition of tossing the bat to the opposing captain once he caught the bat the other player put his hand on the top of the others and so on until they reach the top of the bat the first one to reach the top of the bat with their thumb gets the first good player. It is amazing how far a thumb can stretch when you need it to. "Toss" that bat say's Dale, over goes the bat to Bill. Dale stretches the most and wins. I pick Grelton says Dale.

Bill picks Moses the choosing goes on until only one boy is left and makes for an odd team. Dale speaks up "we take first at bat" who has a glove? We need to have a glove for the catcher at least. Yes, we have one but we only have one ball so keep it out of the tall grass, Eire warns everyone. Now the boys have a long narrow pit where the pitcher has stood so many games. The same goes for home plate a spot is worn out where everyone had stood to bat and catch the ball. The other bases are worn spots on the ground too some grass is trying to grow over the spot the grass will never make it. The game gets started for a while when one by one each boy must go home. Finally only the Bush brothers are there to play "500".

You know how to play 500 you get fifty points for a grounder and you get one hundred points for a fly ball caught before it hits the ground. First man to get 500 points gets to bat the balls out to the others' "Hit some grounders too Erie" Bill yells out.

Finally everyone must go home. The game of baseball for the boys is a passion, dreaming of the heroes of the game for their day. Some player cards are even found in Chillicothe Missouri at the local drug store in their favorite bubble gum pack if they could afford to purchase them.

"Come on Erie" let's get on home the breeze is coming up and the clouds are getting real dark let's go quickly! Bill has lived long enough to recognize the bad signs. As the boy's approach home there is no doubt about what is happening with the weather that evening it is a twister as they called it, it is a tornado. There is an eerie, green look to all of the surrounding area. One of the worst nightmares that can happen in the Midwest is a tornado; usually a tornado will happen in May or June when spring is giving way to summer.

Bill runs in to the house and screams "TWISTER, A TWISTER IS COMING!!

Poppa grabs the baby and tells everyone in a calm voice "head to the root" cellar. As they go outside a wood picket fence that was just painted goes past them going east. There is just enough room, knee to knee to sit down in the root, cellar. Momma lights a candle and starts a song to keep everyone calm. Poppa closes the door behind them. The raw power of the tornado can be heard like the sound of a train. The winds blow more than 200 miles per hour as one of nature's most powerful forces are at work that evening. The tornado has no conscience and is totally unforgiving in the way it destroys but at the same time seems to be very selective once you can access the damage. The Bush family has some water and food they have taken with them. In the cellar are some shelves that have glass jars lined up neatly from the garden canning of last year.

Just as quick as the train, noise of the twister is heard the noise is gone. Poppa slowly opens the big door, and then says "stay here" Poppa goes out to check for damage. It is some time before he comes back "all clear" yells papa you can come up. We have been spared only the hog pen is missing and our front porch posts. The next day brings news of the farm next over East. The Jones have lost their hay barn and all of the animals and there is no trace of them.

That same week on Sunday the men get together and plan the clean-up and rebuilding of the barn for the Jones. People pulling together especially Midwest people will turn around this spring event. Bill will reminisce more of these "growing up" stories as he dreams of home when he is so far away in Turkey and France.

Bill will remember when the family was sick and when his bird dog has a litter of puppies and of course this twister.

FIRST FIGHT

———•———

*I*t must be an ancient Prima donna act, a ritual that must take place in every young boy's life. The first time a boy is challenged and has a fight. There can be many reasons for fighting. Some boys simply have to inflect the same pain they receive at home from their parent who is harsh in punishing. There will always be the need, the implanted character for all boys to find out who is strongest who is fastest, who is the best. Who is the leader of the group? In rural Missouri in the as in all places' there is always a rival group. Now these groups of boys didn't meet up to often but once a year at the county fair all the regional groups of boys would run across each other. Bill, Dale nor Moses would really ever think to pick a fight with anyone. In fact except for some minor scuffles at home none of the group of boys had been in a real out and out fistfight. It is one hot summer night at the county, fair on the midway and two groups meet up and not all is well. The largest of the boys of the other group speaks up out of line. This is the boy who wishes to pass on the pain, his own pain from harsh punishments at home. This boy will challenge whoever he believes he can whip and he has whipped his share. " What do you say Shorty," Who are you speaking to? Asked Dale? "Shorty there" the bully is calling out Bill. Did your mother let you out to play? What can I do for you tonight? Bill answered back.

Bill had a way about himself, first of all Bill had that slow Texas type drawl of speech. Bill really never talked a lot. Bill's Dad had told him this day would come. Where are you from runt? Hey buddy say's Dale to the taller farm boy the larger boy pushes Dale in the chest. Then, out of nowhere Bill flies into the big mouth, boy. First a hit to the noise, then a flurry to the eyes and a knee to the groin area. The taller young man didn't have time to recover when Bill jumps up using both feet to the chest knocking him to the ground. By this time the larger boy is on the ground with a bloody noise. The fight is over. Bill is gentleman enough to help the boy up and others help with the clean-up. There are even introductions and some handshakes. All is well and the groups are on their way for a better time. The first fight for Bill was not much to worry about; Bill could handle himself quite well. Pound for pound Bill is strong and quick a great combination that goes well with being not afraid. God tells us not to be frightened of any man of this earth but be very frightened of the man who can send you to Hell for an eternity.

Matthew 10:28 and *Luke 12:5*. Do not be afraid of those who kill the body but cannot kill the soul rather be afraid of the one who can destroy both soul and body in Hell.

FIRST GIRL FRIEND

———•••———

*D*iscovering girls happens to every boy or young man. This discovery happens to some boys sooner than others but it always happens. I would say that every man alive could remember the first time they realized that there is a difference between boys and girls and they just found someone they are interested in, that first puppy love.

Adam calls her woman because she was taken out of man. In *Genesis 2:23*. In *Genesis 3:20*, Adam, the first man, names her name Eve, because she is the mother of all living.

Boys discovering girls simply happen naturally. One day a boy looks at a girl differently he then decides to like her without really knowing why. All girls will immolate this same ritual and encourage the young man but that is another story.

Now, while this first love Phenomena is going on with the young man there is a change that happens to his personality. I could only guess you could blame it on hormones the boy ignores all other people around him. When you try to talk with him he would hear only about half of the conversation at best. Sometimes you think he is really floating on air above the ground. The boy's brain seems to be somehow become disconnected from his body or simply has no blood going to it. This leaves him brainless. There is only one thought in his head that is the girl. The attention given to the girl friend leaves the other members of the family in the dust so to speak. The mother who would normally have more attention from her son discovers she is still loved but now she isn't the only girl in the young man's life anymore. The same thing goes for Dad, brothers, sisters, grandpa, grandma, who is left? This could be called puppy love, infatuation, first love, but is it love at all? When is it called love? When does it become real love? Very few of these first loves become a lifelong love relationship. Some first loves are even put on hold for 50 and 60 years and then started up again, these now older lovers make the perfect couple they are helpmates for each other for the years they have left here on earth.

Bill Bush doesn't know it yet but he is not immune to this hormonal change in his own personality. It is just going to be delayed a bit because of the war. Bill was always too busy and never found a girl that really turned his head. There was only one time that Bill even halfway notices the person that he will eventually marry. These girls are playing in the sandbox, of all places, at the church, Bill and his friends are walking by they don't even notice these girls much. It is Grace and her friends they are much younger at that time. Grace is still into dolls at that time. Before Bill really has his chance to go for the girls he is off to the War. It will be four long years before he is back and have time for any romantic, relationship. Bill's personal life is on hold because of the current world problems. Bill will soon become Government Issue an Army GI. It is Bill's one brother, Erie that will first become infatuated with his first love. There is huge inconvenience for Erie with this relationship and that is that the girl in question lives the next county over East of Chillicothe, some forty miles away from the Bush family farm. Erie has to find ways to go see this girl. He volunteers to go to town and get supplies or any excuse to leave the farm is thought up. Really nothing can stop the relationship. All parts of the formal courting process will still be observed. A long engagement. There are many rules. One of the most important is the two young people are never be alone with the each other, for any reason. A chaperone is to be present with them at all times.

Before Bill makes it back to the US after the war Erie has been married and has a family.

Be fruitful and multiply *Genesis 9:1* and *Genesis 9:7* Erie and his wife have no problem with that Bible verse. They have twins right off and then one child per year after that till they have a wonderful family of eight. Five boys and three girls.

A LIE AND A PROVERB

*T*he Bush children usually didn't have reason to lie to their parents. One day both of Bills parents decide to go to town at the same time and leave the boys alone for the entire day. Before the parents leave they review the usual chores with them to be accomplished.

Poppa even adds some to ensure they stay busy. Momma and poppa take off for the day and the boy's do well working as they might usually do. Their chores get completed quickly but some bickering starts up. The younger boys are verbally fussing saying one isn't doing their fair share of the work in the house. The all outside chores were completed and poppas extra work, has put all them inside cleaning up. The fussing turns into a pushing match then a friendly wrestling match. It only takes a few minutes when one of them rolls into a lamp stand and breaks it. Then the blaming starts up. You did it you caused it!! They decide to hide the problem and not say who did it. As you may guess the boys didn't fool Momma. How did everything go? Momma asks when she returns. All that it takes is a moment's hesitation and Momma knows something is wrong. "Did anything go wrong boys"? She walks into the front room and sees the rug has been moved and has a bump in it. She scans the room and there is the broken leg of the lamp stand. The boys have lied. Lying is serious.

Many proverbs come in to play this day. Poppa will use discernment in dealing with the boys. First the bible says in *Proverbs 22:15* - Do not withhold discipline from a child.

If you punish him with the rod he will not die. *Proverbs: 23:14*, punish him with the rod and save his soul from death. *Proverbs 19:9* a false witness will not go unpunished and he who pours out lies will perish. *Prov.13: 24* He who spares the rod hates his son, but is careful to discipline him. That will be what Poppa does; he will be careful but must not spare the rod. The boys have been lined up in the front room. Momma and poppa have had a talk away from the boys so they can't hear them talk. It is decided that all will receive the strap twice each. Poppa and Momma know that the boys will never let them know who really did this but all will share in the punishment. "Boys" you know I love you but I must give out some punishment for your actions. You will all help pay for the repair as well. This punishment is not for breaking the lamp stand but is for not telling the truth to your Momma. Lying is bad and God doesn't like a liar. All the boys are turned around and swatted twice the strap stings greatly. "Now get back to your chores" everyone scrambles out the back door in a hurry rubbing their behinds.

SICKNESS COMES

---

*I*t's that time of year, when sickness comes, everyone fears it. Or it could be a bad batch of meat. It is what makes you so sick that you start to talk to God in your weakness. It is easy to talk to God because you are already on your knees. As some of you may know already God is made perfect in our weakness.

The sickness goes on hour after hour all night and half the next day. You empty yourself of all you have and then go past what you can stand. This is what happens to Bill's family no one knows what caused it, the sickness just happens. Most all in the house get it, so no one can help anyone else. This one particular time though Momma doesn't get it. Momma then becomes the Doctor and nurse, Man of the house along with all of her regular duties. Have you ever asked yourself where moms get the energy to do all of what they can accomplish in one day? I know I have. This time Dad gets the sickness the worst. Erie, Bill and Oland get it but bounce back with some resilience after one night. It does take three and four days for Papa to get back to normal and able to eat regular meals. It was saltines and hot tea. Most soda pops that we may use today for an upset stomach, like 7-up didn't get commercially sold until 1929 and only after the pop top was invented to hold in the pressure of the carbonated water in the newly invented glass pop bottle. You have Pepsi-Cola by 1903 in May 1886 Coca Cola, 1885 Dr. Pepper was invented in Waco Texas and introduced at the 1904 World's Fair in St. Louis.

The hotdog bun the hamburger bun and the ice-cream cone were also introduced. In 1893 we get Hires root beer and by 1919 we get A&W root beer. One of the many home remedies involved mixing whiskey, honey, some lemon juice and hot water, thus the "Hot Toddy" was invented. One or two good shots of Yellowstone 100 proof whiskey and you sweat out the bug and you sleep like a baby. I believe we take the healing of our bodies for granted. We cut a finger and have an open wound for a few days then it simply is better somehow. We are made in Gods image he gives healing to us.

Well praise God, in about a week all is back to normal. Momma, for some reason, never got sick. Word does come later that other local families have some of the same problems of being sick.

WORLD EVENTS

orld events finally drag America into the First World War. One of these events happens on our own soil. This attack happens at a place called Black Tom Island in New Jersey. The date is July 30, 1916 approx. 2AM, German saboteurs blow up 100,000 pounds of TNT explosives that were to be shipped to Great Britain for the war effort. The force of the blast was as powerful as a 5.5 earthquake. The explosion sent derby into the Statue of Liberty, base and arm, killed seven people and broke out glass windows miles away. The value of the explosives was the same as 350 million today.

Another event or war act was before the Black Tom Island this On May the 7, 1915 the German U-boat 20, sends a torpedo into the side of the Lusitania, a British ship caring a war effort cargo from America. The sinking took 18 minutes and killed 1,924 people including 114 Americans. U20 was sunk later in the War.

Other events were to take place. In Russia you have a revolution and by July 16th 1918 the Tsar Nicholas ll the Romanov family is murdered.

A man named Vladimir Llich Ulyanov changed his name to V.I.Lenin and led the Bolshevik Party and the revolution. He was a communist or socialist.

A "Bush Family, meeting" took place after some of these events and knowing that War was about to start for America. It is early spring and the heavy farm work had not yet began Poppa gathers all of the family together knowing life is about to change course. "We are of German heritage" says poppa but we are Americans first. We may be hated if people think differently. We need to show we don't agree of what Germany is doing and that war is wrong. As Bill and his siblings listened to their father they knew that sacrifices would need to be made.

After the family meeting Bill made a personal choice to enlist to fight for America. Bill would have to travel down from Breckenridge, Missouri to Chillicothe so he could enlist. Chillicothe was a larger town with more services because of the train station that is located there.

As you may expect there is another story this about enlistment, no one has heard. Bill and only one of his brothers, Oland was of age to go to war. The problem Bill and Oland had was that one of them was needed to stay back and help run the family farm and rock quarry, business.

It was odd how they made the joint decision of who would go to serve. Of the two brothers, Bill was of a more thin build and could run much faster. Bill's speed in running became the deciding factor on who would go to war. After much prayer, the two brothers made the trip to Chillicothe together to get Bill enlisted. It would be almost four full years before Oland would see Bill again. For Bill, it would be the same number of long years before he would again see Oland or any of his family and friends or those wheat fields of home. A sea of wheat grows in the Midwest and it is a beautiful sight every June when the breeze blows gently through the fields. That breeze makes those gentile, golden waves sway back and forth looking, just like the ocean surface water.

As friendships go you couldn't get a more tightly knit group of friends than the local boys, now they are young men from Chillicothe and Breckenridge Missouri. As soon as Moses Johnson found out that Bill had enlisted, he and his brother, Otis, head straight down to enlist themselves so as not to break the group. The boys are just of acceptable age to go serve. Younger brother Otis wants to go but he is told to wait two more years to make eighteen, the legal age. These are true friends that love each other. The Bible has some verses that describe perfectly what a friend is. Jesus had a friend he loved, his name was Lazarus. *John 11:11.* Job had a friend named Elihu.

Sometimes friends must tell you things you don't wish to hear. *Proverbs 18:24* there is a friend who sticks closer than a brother. *Proverbs 27:6* Wounds from a friend can be trusted. David had a good friend in Jonathan, who saved his life.

The enlistment officer assures the friends that they could stay together but not all was true they were told it's the Army way. The first problem is that Moses is Negro. A black, in today's way of speaking.

The prejudices back then were not settled. Negro's are considered as servants or of lesser value, this is how even the Army looked upon Moses.

The young men go back to their respective homes for two days and then need to report back, they have been sworn into service for America. It is time to go to what is now called boot camp, for military training.

It is departure day for the young men leaving for war. The train station is crowed down in Chillicothe some girls are giving away cookies and Grace is one of the Girls. "Thank you" says Bill in that slow Texas type draw he had, as the young Grace, only a girl really, gives him some yummy oatmeal cookies, and Bill says 'thank you again"

A band has come out to play for the sendoff of the now group of men who have joined up. People are waving and crying and hugging and kissing. Everyone is saying good bye. Some of the good byes will be for good. All of the Bush family is there to see Bill and his friends leave.

The train pulls out with a slow pull of steam, energy and a loud blast or two from the conductor and his whistle. The train chugs slowly, away as people wave and yell their farewell's another blast or two goes out loudly. This train will go down to Kansas City, Missouri to the new Union station about one hundred ten miles to the south and West of Chillicothe. Once there, the men will take another troop train down to Fort Funston or modern day, Fort Riley in the middle of the state of Kansas, the Sunflower State.

Bill and Moses start on their three hour train trip to Kansas City only to find out that they will have a ten hour layover before they leave again. All of the other incoming trains need to deliver their load of men. The boys are in complete awe of the Union station Building.

There is a breath taking sight as you enter the Grand Hall of the train station in Kansas City. A ninety- five foot tall ceiling with a six foot diameter clock hanging in the train station's central archway. The North waiting room alone holds ten thousand people and is mostly full. The whole complex is ten levels nine hundred rooms and has 850,000 square feet of space. It takes the boys hours to check out the different restaurants and shops in the building. At its prime in 1917 the station had 271 trains go through in one day, 79,368 trains that year alone.

The boys didn't know it then but the Liberty Memorial would be built directly across from the Union station by 1926. This is the only monument in the United States dedicated to the men and women who died during the First World War. Both buildings will undergo extensive renovation ninety some years later.

Wow!! What a place! Exclaims Bill and Moses at nearly the same time. This place is really smooth, the top banana!!! I would not want to clean this place though, say's Moses. The boys are in a temporary euphoria and the mood gets even better when a familiar face comes walking across the huge and crowded, Union Station floor, it is Dale Bird. The old friend is looking good and is still as happy a personality as he ever was. It is hugs all round for the reunion of old friends it has been four and one half years since Dale and his family moved to Kansas City, Missouri.

Alleluia, happy days! How are you? What are you doing here?

They all speak at once. A flurry of questions starts up when Dale says, what does it look like? I joined up the very same as you. I couldn't let you have all the glory!! The young men didn't notice some lovely girls that went closely by them. Dale tells his friends "My Dad worked on this building it is just opened. Dad did some of the plastering work up on the ceiling. They all look up some 95 feet I was down here with him some days when I could be.

The young men reminisce together of when they played baseball and so many good times they enjoyed together. Dale asks how everyone is doing back in Chillicothe and Breckenridge. The mood gets a little somber, they now know life is changing and maybe not for the better. What do you think camp will be like? Moses asked Dale, I hope the food will be good. There is much laughter among the group.

Time is going past quickly and it is nearing the departure time they were told by their Sergeant. They go to the new Harvey restaurant that is just off the grand hall of the depot and have a quick, bite of food and drink. "We had better get going" Bill says with some authority in his voice. They leave and go to the huge waiting room and down the stairs to board the train. It will be a long nights traveling. The young friends continue to talk for half of the night and finally hit the sack about 3:30 a.m.

The train comes to a slow stop, "everyone up" yells the Sergeant. Make ready to fall out in front of the station. This station is a far cry from the one in Kansas City, Missouri. "It looks more like home", exclaims Moses yes I agree said Bill. All of these smaller stations had a woman's and a men's side to them where the men go smoke and the women were just considered women. There isn't any women's right's movement yet. That will not happen until after the war when women win the right to vote by 1926.

Up in the wagon, "get cracking" yell's the Sergeant. Horse and wagon was still a common method of transportation for most of all rural America. And the United States Army was no different using both horse and mule for the work of moving man and equipment. Moses is employed immediately to help drive one of the teams. Bill helps with some gear storage and each man's work become defined quickly, the Quarter Master Corp.

Considering Moses and his family had a farm and fertilizer hauling business he was more than used to handling a team of mules and a wagon.

Bill was a farmer and his family had a rock quarry business. Later on, during the War Bills ability to speak the German language fluently would send him to a place long forgotten about.

No one knows where Dale Bird is stationed and is not heard from for many years. Basic training starts early the next day, 4AM sharp a loud blast on a whistle from the drill instructor. "FALL OUT "Hit the Deck!! LET'S GO!! You all have 20 minutes to have your showers make yours beds and be in formation for inspection in front of this hut.

The Drill instructor, Jessie Stales, starts the discipline that morning early and it will carry through till "his boys" leave for Europe. Jessie takes personal responsibility for all of the men under his direction for the next six weeks. Jessie directs the men by doing the exercises himself. We are going to start with callisthenic exercises each morning starting with jumping jacks, then up and downs, sit ups, and finally push-ups. There will be a five mile run after we have this warm up time. Every day, rain or shine for the next three weeks everyone gets in good physical condition. Finally after the two per day workouts there is time for hand to hand combat training and they get out on the firing range.

Bill and most everyone does well with the training. It is said that an army runs on its stomach, Supplies will be organized for the shipping from a port in New Orleans, Louisiana going to a port in France.

Each man is issued all his field gear, full pack with bedroll, and a Springfield model .300 rifle. The side arm was a 1911, .45 caliber, semiautomatic pistol. No steel, metal helmet was issued out because America didn't have a helmet for the troops until the fall of 1917. British helmets were issued for the troops there in France. Some 400,000 were given out. By the end of the Great War the US M-1917 steel helmet as they called it, weighing two pounds each, had reached production of 2,707,237 from various companies and they were all painted by the Ford motor company. The paint had sawdust in it to help the finish be dull and not reflect light.

Most of the troops travel back to New Jersey. From there they will load ship and sail across the Atlantic going to England first then on to France for. This will take the better part of month to accomplish.

Moses and Bill are shipping out of New Orleans. They will be in charge of supplies like c-rations, ammunition. There will be animals necessary to pull the wagons and the caissons. Horses and mules, Moses is in charge of them. "Quarter Master" Bill and Moses are off to The Great War as it became known. Once all the troops made it to France there was much work to do in deploying out to the "Front".

The battle action was immediate and welcomed by the allies. Bill and Moses find out they have lots of new equipment and weapons to disperse. Within days their pivotal encounter with the Enemy is totally by accident. The two men have a huge wood, wagon loaded with ammunition and weapons. Driving the team of horses they don't realize they have driven right up to the right flank of the German defenses. They are spotted and they are still on the wagon like sitting ducks. The wood chips start filing off the seat as they jump off to the ground from enemy, bullets. Bill causally, says to Moses in his usual slow Texas, drawl. "What do we have with us for weapons"? Moses says, we have those new Thompson machines!! Let me try one says Bill, still calmly speaking.

Moses tosses Bill one. A group of six Germans is coming up a low grade toward them shooting. Bill steps out and begins blasting away. Moses sees Bills bravery and comes out boldly the same. These Germans are no match but a larger number on Germans are coming faster now. Bill and Moses are over run and it gets down to hand to hand combat because all the solders are out of ammunition. Moses is a very strong man he takes on two men at once and Bill has the last one. Bill remembers he has a knife at his boot top and the encounter is over after a short while. Bill and Moses have killed more than thirty German soldiers.

They both sit up against a wagon wheel and are exhausted but they are not hurt badly. We need to leave here Moses says and "praise the Lord for those new guns". A quick prayer is said thanking God for getting them through the Battle.

It is back to supplying the troops for a while but as the word got around of what Moses and Bill had done there was a call up for a special assignment.

Both men were called back to high command. Once the command officers were aware the Moses was a black man he was sent straight back to his front line job.

"They claim you killed a number a Germans in a short battle is that true"? Bill is always slow to speak "Yes Sir" "Can you understand and speak the German, Language"? "Ja" (German word for English yes). "Would you have any problems being resigned for a special assignment"? "Nein" again German for "no". There is another officer there that could also speak German. This officer begins a conversation in German, with Bill that lasts for a few minutes. After that, the officer says "he will do just fine". The commander speaks, "Bill we need an interpreter and someone with some grit to gather information for us in Turkey". "We require information about troop strength and enemy, army locations".

"Can you be ready by 01200 tomorrow"? "Yes Sir". Bill finds out about Moses only after the talks and is saddened. He bids good bye to his friend that next morning. They will not see each other for more than a year and a half.

THE GERMAN

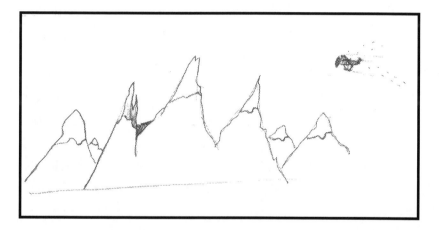

The old man tells his story but the attendants at the nursing home just outside of Munich, Germany pay little attention to him. The man is 102 years old now and the year is 1997. Surprisingly the old man can still walk and has a full head of hair. His hair color is a yellowish, white. He can walk but it is more like a shuffle but give him credit, he is a centurion and more. He shares a room with a man much younger who looks older than him. "I seen it" the old man tells his story in the German language "I was in it" sure Otto we believe you. The attendants pacify the old man. "Yes Otto" you seen the ark. The old airman has out lived all his friends and most of his own family.

Now, one relative a great, great grandson has looked up the older relative remembering him from when he was a little boy himself. The day has come to visit and Rudy makes the trip from Berlin. Hello Otto, do you remember me? I was only a boy when I saw you last. The old man stares at him for a long while "you are Rudy". "Yes" I'm Rudy your great, great Grandson. It was remarkable the old German still had all his wits about him and a sound mind. Hello sorry I haven't come before now to visit you says Rudy. Rudy speaks in German also. "Rudy, I must tell you of what I seen during the war". "The war,"? Said Rudy with a question. Yes, during the Great War. I need to tell you, Otto says, with much emotion in his voice, what I saw. Rudy understands the urgency of listening to him. Yes, I have time Grandpa I have time for you and I believe you. Rudy is ready to listen when a nurse comes in with Otto's twice-daily medications. After she is gone Otto continues, I need to tell you what I did see in the country of Turkey. I saw the ark, Noah's ARK! Rudy is still for a moment. He has to take that statement in and not be disrespectful to his recently found relative.

The ark? The wooden ship? Yes. Where? How? When? Rudy has heard of a Bible story but the reality of a real Ark is a shock to him. Please Grandpa, you need to start over here, from the beginning. I want to believe you Grandpa. I haven't been going to church regularly. The old man is tired and it is close to dinnertime. Otto sighs and says, this will take some time young man, have you got the time for it? Yes, you really have my attention now. Please, let me get some paper and pencil to take down some notes. Otto starts by asking Rudy a question or two. Rudy did you know I was born in 1885? No, I didn't says Rudy, I must tell you Grandpa I know little about you or your life. I don't know much about what happened during the War or why there was a war either. Otto continues, I had only seen an air machine once or twice before myself and my new friend Von Richthofen was to be trained to fly one.

We were trained on the Albatross D1 and the Fokker's DR1 tri plane. Grandpa, I didn't even know you flew a plane. Otto remembers, I met some Americans and British soldiers. An Airmen and one American foot soldier in particular named Bill. He was with me when I went back on the ground to find the ARK. Rudy speaks up, they would be witnesses to what you're telling me about? I would think them all to be dead by now, Otto tells him.

After my training I was sent to France. The War was at a standstill on the ground. It had become a trench War. Mostly we were to spot the movements of the ground troops and report back to our forces. We would run into the British AVRO 504K planes once in a while.

I was in France for nearly two years losing many friends before being assigned to go to Turkey. Since you don't know, the Ottoman Empire or the country of Turkey was an ally to Germany during the Great War. We called them "Turks" without any explanation I was transferred to Turkey.

Why was there a war? You ask me, Rudy, poverty, we all lived in desperate, unforgiving, poverty. I also need to tell you that there were many inventions of the era that were changing how men looked at war and fighting. The inventions allowed for more efficient ways of killing and gave them confidence. In 1898 Georg Lugar and Hugo Borchardr two German inventors invented the German Lugar automatic pistol and the Mouser automatic pistol respectively. In America John Browning in 1911 invents the .45 caliber automatic pistol. The gun is still standard issue for the US military today. The one invention that would change my life was the airplane. Invented in 1903 in America by the Wright brothers (they made bicycles before that) the first flight was 169 linear feet. They flew at Kitty Hawk, North Carolina, where ever that is.

As you can know by now Rudy not all inventions are used for the betterment of mankind. Modern warfare came about with the inventions. Planes, bombs, toxic gas, and as you can imagine, the new automatic pistols and machine guns. It is obvious you can improve almost anything as you have a "need" as the saying goes, "Necessity, is the Mother of invention". I believe men will always have a "need" for better weapons then countries can use the improved weapons to engage in War.

I would have settled for electric lights. Lights were still new in 1891 and installed in the US White House. Where as I understand the American President at the time was afraid to turn then on for fear of being shocked or electrocuted.

Do you want more history Rudy? Do you mean how did the War start up? Yes, I have plenty of time to listen. The War also came down to ideals and varying, ethnic groups in differing countries. It was July 28th 1914 when Austria- Hungary declares War on Serbia two days later Russia mobilized troops to support Serbia. On August 1st Germany declares war on Russia It was downhill after that. France declares war on Russia. Germany declares war on France. Great Britain declares war on Germany, Austria and Hungary declare war on Russia. Serbia then declares war on Germany. Great Britain declares war on Austria- Hungary. By August the 23rd Germany invades France. Japan jumps in and declares war on Germany. Turkey enters in on the German side. Russia then declares war on Turkey. France also declares war on Turkey. You must remember that Turkey was then part of the Ottoman Empire. After World War I there was no more Ottoman Empire. The Ottoman Empire was once the mightiest empire on earth next to the Roman Empire. The United States would be drawn into the war after the sinking of the civilian ocean, liner, Lusitania. By April 6th 1917 President, Woodrow Wilson declares war on Germany for the United States. After that, some German saboteurs went into New Jersey, USA at Black Tom Island and blew up a munitions storage depot.

I found myself transferred to a place called Megiddo. In the valley of Jezreel. This is the same valley that will be the gathering place of the army of the Anti- Christ. Anti-Christ? Who is that? That will be the Army who fights the "last battle" on earth. "The battle of Armageddon" Are you still with me Rudy? Yes, Grandpa I will get a Bible and read it. We became reinforcements and air support for the Turks. We knew that the Americans were coming to help fight against us, (Germany). Our squadron of five planes total, were sent down from France, in hopes to save Bagdad from being taken by the French and British troops. As we were on our way, we were flying over the Ararat Mountains. We were going to follow the Euphrates River down to Bagdad. I simply had looked down at a glance of a shape that was out of place for the mountains.

Rudy, as much as I want to finish telling you all about what happens, can you come back tomorrow? I'm very tired now. "Yes Grandpa". Otto had gone as far with the story as he could for one day. Otto spoke very, slowly anyway and the time had flown by it is 10:30 at night and everyone else at the nursing home is in bed. Rudy says his "Guten Abend" to Otto and heads for the hotel. Rudy has on his mind all of what Otto had been telling him about, the ark, Armageddon, Anti- Christ, this was all deep thought for someone not going to church regularly. Rudy says to himself what is the old man talking about?

Rudy needs a Bible and quickly. The Bible is the one true history book of where man is going and where he has been.

The next day, Rudy is a little late getting back to see Otto because he stops off at the local bookstore. The vendor immediately asks back, what Bible do you want Sir?

Do you want a King James, New King James, NIV? NIV? Rudy asks quickly. "New International Version" explains the vendor. I have more. You must be new are you recently saved? I have a King

41

James, beginners, study Bible you could try. OK, I'll purchase that one.

Rudy is more prepared for Otto today. He has his new Bible and a better pad of paper. When Rudy arrives at the nursing home he gets alarmed, there is much going on, one of the patients across from Otto is having a bad time, something is wrong. They are taking this person out for care.

Guten Morn Rudy!! Otto is an early riser and has been all of his life. Have you had any breakfast yet Rudy? I have some biscuits and gravy left if you want some. Thank you, I will finish those. Thank you Grandpa. Before Rudy was finished Otto says, "Did you know I was captured during the Great War? I was a prisoner after the battle at Meggaddo. The Turks lost you know. The Ottoman Empire was no more after that battle and the war ended.

When the battle started we were doing well I had shot down one plane going for another when two of them were on my tail. I did my best. I shot down another when I was hit and started to smoke. I managed to land and was immediately picked up by the other forces right away. The war was over for me after that. But Grandpa you said you was inside the ark. "Hold on Rudy"!

I was taken to a headquarters and questioned this is when I met the American named Bill. He could speak German as well as I can. He asked all the questions, I cooperated and answered him.

Later, when I could, I asked the American how he knew German so well. He told me of where he was from and who his parents were and he told me what it was like in America. He talked funny. Someone told me he talked like a Texican, whatever that is.

I can tell you Rudy; America must be a wonderful place. I asked this American if he knew of Noah's Ark. He said yes. Can we stop here Grandpa? Will you tell me the story of Noah? The ark? "Yes I can Rudy the story is in that new bible you have." You will need to read this book completely for yourself just so you know.

Let me start with who Noah is related to. Noah had a famous grandfather his name was Methuselah he was the oldest living man at 969 years old. Noah's father was Lamech, he lived 777 years.

Noah himself had lived 500 years when he had his sons Shem, Ham and Japheth. Started building the ark.

God had made a decision based on man's wicked ways to destroy all whom lived in the earth. He told this to Noah who God chose to keep a covenant with. God found that Noah was a righteous man and blameless among all the people keeping the faith.

Noah is instructed to build an ark to hold two of every creature both male and female. Every kind of bird and animal that moves along the ground. Noah is also to take every kind of food to be stored for food for himself and the animals.

Now this task of the ark will take some time for the boys and Noah to build and to pitch both inside and outside as instructed by God. There will only be one door in the ark and God himself will shut it when time comes.

As I said Rudy it will take some time to build this ark, Noah will be 600 years old when it is ready. The ark is 450 feet long 75 feet wide and 45 feet tall. There are three decks finished to within 18 inches of the top.

For seven days Noah and his family and their family's entered the ark. The animals entered the ark with God's help. Then, as God had told Noah, a great flood will start. For forty days and forty nights the flood gates of the heavens opened and the springs of the deep burst open. It rained and flooded the entire earth killing all living things and people. After one hundred and fifty days the God remembered Noah and the animals in the ark. Noah tested with birds to see if there was land. Noah sends out a raven but there is no proof. Later Noah sends out a dove with the same result. Finally after seven days, Noah sends out another dove and it returns with a fresh cut olive leaf. God then sent a wind to resin the floodwaters. When the waters had gone down the ark came to rest on the mountains of Ararat.

When Noah is six hundred and one years old the waters had dried up. Noah then removed the door from the ark and God told him to come out.

Noah then builds an altar and sacrificed burnt offerings to the Lord God.

Rudy, God made a covenant not to destroy the earth by flood again and that covenant is, his rainbow set in the sky by God himself.

Noah lived another 350 years after the flood and died at the age of 950 years old.

I don't believe we will live nearly that long grandpa.

You are wrong Rudy. We just won't live on this earth that long but we can have eternal life if we only believe in Jesus the Lord of all. I have left out some details of this story like what happens after the flood so you really need to read for yourself the full account.

This American, Bill was a man who knew the story of Noah and about the Ark . I told him of what I had noticed coming over the mountains. This man knew this was important. We talked more. Bill was thinking, this has been a very hot summer even for this area one of the hottest in over 100 years. This may explain why you could see such a thing.

We must go back and look for the Ark. The problem is we are miles from there, and I'm a prisoner of war. Now it is September and soon the winter will start in the mountain areas. Fortunately, the mission was accomplished for this American, and the British group they had come to help fight but also gather information about troop strength in the area. After we lost the battle all of the Turks that were left ran away and disbanded. I was one of just a few prisoners. The American and the Brit decide to have me take them back to the mountains and try to find the Ark from the ground. They trusted me for some reason, I guess no one could come up with a story like I had told them. We had to travel up the Euphrates River, going back toward the Ararat Mountains. We were given provisions and camels to ride by the Arabians. They were on the American and British side of things

As our group traveled we had to go West over to the Tigris River and more North along the mountains. The terrain was much harder to recognize from the ground and we were a long way from being high enough.

We traveled toward the ancient runes of Nineveh by the Euphrates River. As you know Nineveh is close to the foot hills of the Ararat, Mountains. We came upon an Oasis named "Kharga". We were very tired and thirsty so we stopped and rested and drank water in the shade for some time. Bill sees a new puppy and remembered and shared of when they had new puppies at home In Missouri. Everyone was excited about the news of the expectant litter. "My dog Pepper" was going to have puppies that summer. The male sire dog of the pups was from a distant farm in Nicodemus, Kansas. This dog was tall, pure breed; German shorthaired whose owner just happened to like hunting pheasant's. The dog owner's name was Mr. Ball a black gentleman. Mr. Ball's payment for the siring of the pups would be the choice of one of the new puppies when they were weaned. As the summer went on Pepper would look huge as though she would have twenty pups. Peppers time finally comes and it takes hours to have the pups. Ten total puppies are born but one dies right away. The mid July temperatures of over 100 degrees everyday put a lot of stress on Pepper. Of the remaining nine pups there is one runt that is almost all chocolate in color. Most all of the rest have beautiful brown and white "ticking" and large to small chocolate spots on them. One larger male becomes my favorite. The new puppies have that new puppy smell to them and you just want to hold them all of the time. I remember Oland yelling in excitement "come quick"!!! The puppies are here!!!!!

Pepper looked as though she never had any food for days all of her ribs were showing. The excitement of the new litter traveled fast.

One day a neighbor comes over who may be interested in owning one of the dogs. I remember we put all the pups in an apple basket. What a sight that was all those dogs squirming around making all those puppy noises of whimpering. They are all loveable and huggable. The neighbor can't decide but said he would be back. When the day came for Mr. Ball to come and get his puppy we were all sad. It doesn't take long before you get attached to the pups. To make it worse Mr. Ball took the dog I really wanted. The dog I did get was a female. That dog had endless energy and a great nose. The noise of the gun going off didn't bother her at all.

All of the other pups were pledged out, by the time they are three weeks old. They were whined at eight weeks old and were gone soon after. A good dog is hard to find much like good friends don't you think? Bill asked me. I didn't answer.

When we were refreshed, we traveled on and made it to Nineveh where we inquired for any guides that could help us with an easy way up the mountains going toward the higher elevations of Ararat. We came across an old man who looked as old as Nineveh itself. He had deep furrows in his face and only one or tooth that you could see. He was smoking a large wooden pipe and was sitting in the doorway to his home. He was dressed as most with a turban on his head. To our surprise, he asked us if we were looking for, as he called it, "the great ship".

The old man said, go quickly not much time left. We were stunned from his statements. I have not seen it since I was a young boy. But this summer is as hot as that same summer. The old man warns us we will need heavy clothing for the cold we will soon face. We took the advice and traded for some pelts. The old man was able to draw out a crude map of how to traverse the mountains to start the journey. With a stone face the old man said, 'it will be hard, you may not come back.

The American, Bill and all of us took the old man seriously." I can send my young, Grandson, Jonah, to guide you some of the way but he will need to come back". I love the boy too dearly and he is the only one who takes care of this old, old man. After all the advice from the old man we had to ask him what did you see? It is close to ancient town. Ancient Town? Yes, you will find the great ship close to ancient town. You must go now, you have not time before the ice comes.

With that statement we started out along an ancient caravan, trading route close to the Ararat, Mountain's with the guide we were given. I could only remember that what I saw from my plane was the image that was far back in the mountains.

Rudy, I'm getting hungry and it is nearly dinner time now. Yes, Grandpa. I will come back tomorrow. Rudy never had any plan to stay this extended time but the story is to intriguing and if this adventure is true, the idea of going back is implanted in own mind now.

The next day is Sunday and Rudy will take Otto out for dinner right after Church service. The weather is good and Otto is able to walk enough to make the trip. Rudy is now anxious to hear more from his Grandpa. As they have dinner Otto tells Rudy about his wife who has long been gone some twenty years and Otto still is missing her very much. "She was beautiful you know" My Hanna. She had green, eyes and sandy, blond hair and was very voluptuous.

I have a picture of her. It is only in black and white. "Yes"!! She is beautiful, Grandpa you are a lucky man. Yes, and we loved each other very much. Hanna and I are only separated by death for a short while. We will be together for an eternity in heaven, when I get there.

Rudy then asks his long lost relative and Great Grandpa "how do you get to go to Heaven? You must believe in the Lord in your heart and professing with your lips that he is Lord. Would you like to pray the salvation prayer now Rudy? "YES' Grandpa I want to go to heaven. Roman's 10:9 That if you profess with your mouth that Jesus is Lord, and believe in your heart that God raised him from the dead you will be saved. For it is with your heart that you believe, and with your mouth that you confess, and are saved." That very day Rudy was saved. "Praise God!!! What a day!! You are a new person now Rudy. Rudy is crying and Otto is too, both in joy and happiness.

Well, Rudy I would guess you wish to hear what happened in the mountains yes?

Otto says. "Yes", Rudy says nearly impatiently now. We left our camels and took lama's these animals are more suitable for the mountainous terrain. We had not gone far when Bill stopped and yelled out mountains!!! The man had never seen the mountains. Bill was, as he called himself a," flatlander". Where I come from we only have bumps on the ground, Bill said. We are all in awe of the range ahead of us. Look! Some have snow on them. As we grew closer to the mountain range the going gets tougher. The shear height of the cliffs dwarfs us as though we were ants. These mountains seemingly just abruptly start up from the flat land. We travel further in and see nothing but more mountains. One mountain hides another and another. Our guide, Jonah turned back for home and left us on our own, he had already went too far with us.

The weather was turning much colder and clouds were going past quickly overhead. We are trapped by a storm for two days in a cave. The British man was getting sick from the thin air and had to stop and turn back leaving only myself and Bill.

We traveled up and much higher and finally came to a place where we could see down a great and vast valley between two mountains. There! "Otto yells out" "Look, up higher do you see it? See the snow is blowing off a drift from it? It took Bill a minute to spot what I was pointing to make it out. This area is an enormously wide, huge valley and another mountain range over. We could only look across the valley' from our mountain. The height up and shearness of the cliff, a spot no one was going to ever traverse.

Then Bill points in amazement "What is that? Pointing down to a frozen, man-made, structure that is below the Ark location. The massive snow and ice crusted, building is closer to the valley floor and looks more like a defensive, fort wall. Bill the "Yank" and I started to climb down our side of the mountain toward the other side. It is just as arduous and treacherous of a decent as going up the mountain it is slow and dangerous because all of the rocks are as huge as a train's, boxcar.

We might have made better time going across that valley floor but the wind was so severe that it was pushing us backward as we walked. The wind never stopped blowing till we were closer to the opposite side. The wind is calmer now but there are some snowflakes whirling about and the temperature is definitely going down.

We picked our way up through the rocks toward these awesome doors. Standing in front of them now and we are simply dwarfed by them. Just one side of the pair is 10 feet wide and 15 feet tall. There is no apparent, visible way of opening them up either.

Are you listening to me Rudy? Yes Grandpa!! This is more than fascinating keep going!!! That must have been accent town the old man was telling you about.

Bill decided to follow the perimeter of the wall. Close to the corner he noticed a trail up the steep cliff. There are footsteps carved into the solid rock, cliff face. The steps disappear in a fog half way up the mountain. We now also see that a huge boulder has crashed in to the wall at some time and allows us a way into the compound. We are seeking some shelter and rest for a while so we entered through the wall breach.

Can I tell you I have never seen such thick of timber as the wall and the buildings were made from. The idea that that much timber could be used as building material seemed odd because we were so far up above the timber line on any mountain. Once inside we find what looks like a monastery or a place of worship and see other smaller building like houses. All of the structures had surfaces that were peeling some sort of thick dark material revealing the wood underneath. Finally, we are out of the wind completely and find a place of rest. Inside one of the smaller buildings there are some beds piled high with old animal furs everything is dusted with a light layer of snow. The center of the main room has a large, round, fireplace and a round hood and chimney going through the roof. What is left of the day's daylight is streaming through the cracks of the house.

We settle in for a night of sleep thinking that the next day Bill and I are going up that carved trail to see what we made the trip for in the first place to see NOAH'S ARK.

I fall sleep with Bill telling me more about the United States. I was always curious and asked him to tell me more. His home State is called Missouri and his hometown is "Breckenridge" I never did tire of him talking about his home life and his family in Missouri. We awaken the next morning and find ourselves hungry with little food left. The trip has taken longer than expected and the weather is turning worse. This day will be our only chance to scale up.

Treacherous is the word for the carved footsteps going up toward the Ark.

The American and I slip occasionally and decide to tie a rope to each other; this proves to be a good decision. This trail is as most mountain trails go, they zigzag, cutting back and forth 180 degree's where you can reach up and touch the next person ahead of you on their boot if you wish too. Luckily we had common sense enough to make and take some hiking poles with us. Up higher we go and approach nearly even to the Great Ship but it is still a good half day's climb away, the trail curves to the left toward the wreck. What we see is the broken middle of the ship most of it packed with snow. The top edge is where the drift is blowing out. Part of the side is missing where we could enter in. Carefully Bill goes ahead of me. Once inside we discover a hole in the floor and a floor above us and a floor below us. There is evidence of animal stalls with straw bales. Considering just half of the ARK was 225 feet long we only explored part of it on two levels and were afraid to do any more. We could not stay long only about an hour, knowing the trip down will be even more dangerous. Bill again leads me out and down back the same way we came up, on the carved footsteps. If I didn't say it was windy let me say it now. I can't remember any wind, to this day as strong as the wind up on that mountain. That night when we made it back we decided this trip must end and we would go back to finish the War.

The next day did bring some surprises. We ventured into the larger building to see what we could and behold it really was a place of worship. There were benches and up front was a thick, flat stone altar. It is time to leave and we both turn to go out when I stopped because I see an amazing site. The wooden lentil above the wide doorway shows a decorative carved edge design. In the center of this beam is carved the name, NOAH and it is very legible. After staring at this for some time we chip off two wood blocks from the doorframe, one for each of us and head back. Bill and I were enemies at war against each other, now we are friends who have bonded. This has been an experience of a lifetime. We make a pact to say nothing to anyone until we are old and about to pass on to glory. We didn't believe that anyone could believe such a story anyway. As soldiers we were in great physical condition. The trip took all of our strength and some we had to pray for, just to make it back to the desert. Bill simply let me go my own way when we got back. It took me several months to walk back home to Germany by then the War was fully over.

Rudy, I didn't expect to live this long life. Most of my friends are long deceased I'm happy to see you and tell you this story. In my belongings at home in the attic you will find a carved wood block. It is the same block that I took from the building door frame. I had taken time to carve it into the likeness of the ark.

Bill had taken a block too. Rudy, you can have my house. Thank you, Grandpa. Rudy is humbled by the gift of the home and thankful.

Otto goes on, it was easily discerned that all of the materials that were used for the wall and structures that we found up there, were beams reused from the ship, the Ark.

There was no other way to get such materials up that high in the mountains. The black peeling material on the wood was the pitch that Noah and his sons Shem, Ham and Japheth had applied to the surfaces of the ark as per God's instructions, once it was completed. Genesis 6:14 "God gave Noah all the instruction's and dimensions for the Ark. God walked with Noah and found him to be righteous and blameless among his people".

The amount of materials required the build the ark would justify what we found we called the place the "city of wood".

I have to tell you Rudy that being inside of the Ark is a humbling and holy experience indeed. There was a silence inside the Ark like none you may have ever thought of but standing there you know that when the Ark was used much life was inside. Life that was being spared by the Lord. It was the evil in the world that the Lord was dealing with in his way.

There is a promise from the Lord that he would never flood the world ever again. He put a permanent sign in the sky, a rainbow to show his word is good and he really does love the world and all in his world.

God just expects, and demands respect. He tolerates disobedience with patience before taking action or giving correction as required. His Patience has an end. God found only one man, in the entire known world to be considered righteous and he was Noah.

Noah was spared from the flood along with his family. The Ark was built with the direction of God's own hand. Otto continues as Rudy is writing down most all the old airman says. "That is my story of what happened while I was away in World War One. I tried to go back to war in the 1940's but they just put me to work in a factory making bullets. We were all nearly bombed and killed by the American's before that war was stopped. You have to hand it to the American's they do win most of the wars they fight in. My house keys are in that draw Rudy. My daughter is gone to heaven ten years ago. Don't worry about coming back here if you don't want to. "I will come back Grandpa"

Rudy makes it back six months later only to find Otto as he was before. It was a good visit. I have changed a lot since finding the Lord tells Rudy. Thank you, Grandpa, Thank you. That next year Otto goes on to be with the Lord himself.

THE WAR IS OVER

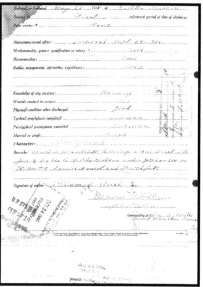

Bill's Honorable Discharge papers from the Army at Fort Funston, Kansas. Stating Bill was of "good character".

T he Great War came to an end on November 11, 1918 they called that day Armistice Day. The war with Germany ended with the signing of the "Treaty of Versailles". The signing date was June 28, 1919.

Bill makes it back to his original unit after the adventure in the Ararat, Mountains. He spends some time in the cold wet trench fighting before the war ends.

Bill is at the departure docks in France now and two old friends are about to be reunited. "BILL", "BILL" it is Moses Johnson yelling having spotted his friend. It has been more than a year and a half since Bill was sent off on the special assignment. "MOSES" The two men find a way to hug each other. Both yell at the same time "you made it' "your alive". They are both amazed at the other being alive after all they have seen and been through. "We can go home," Moses says, "can you believe it"?

Moses needs to share something, "Bill, I got a letter from home, and my brother has been sent to prison in Leavenworth, Kansas". "He was convicted of raping a white girl. He says no way, he didn't do it". Bill says, "I'm sorry to hear this we know he is innocent". "He is a good Christian boy".

The men say a prayer on the spot and then need to get back to work. Moses notices that Bill doesn't look too good. "I don't feel the best and I have a bad cough too". Bill doesn't know he has walking pneumonia. He won't be walking when he gets off the troop ship. The conditions in the troop ship close quarters and cold helps to bring on double pneumonia. He will be carried off the ship. The long train trip home is no help for Bills health and by the time he is back in Kansas City at the Union Station, Bill is very bad.

The only thing the long trip home will help with is "decompressing" from battle fatigue. Talking to fellow solders helps pass time and settle the nerves over the many battles, noise and sights of battle.

There is a great parade in Kansas City, Missouri for all the returning solders in front of the Union Station. Bill is on a stretcher.

It is a grand day but hard to celebrate for Bill. Moses is a true friend and stays with Bill and sends him off on another train ride but not to home. Bill is sent back to Camp Funston, modern day Fort Riley in Kansas, for recovery. Bills recovery will take eight months. The VA or Veterans Administration had not been created yet. It will take a great demonstration in Washington D.C. of hundreds of vets to start the Veterans administration and for the boys to get all their deserved benefits.

Moses has seen Bill off from Union station and is preparing to board for home when he spots a familiar person, he thinks. Yes, it is Dale Bird but he has changed. As Moses gets closer to him he realizes that Dales face has been mutilated on one side and one arm is missing. "Dale" "how is a" exclaims Moses, in his way of speech. "You made it"!

"Hi Moses", Dale's usual happy personality has been replaced with a more subdued and serious persona. "I see you made it to". Dale immediately asks about Bill. "Where is Bill"?

"Did he make it"? "Yes, he did but he is very sick with the pneumonia". "He's gone to get better at camp".

Moses asks, "How long have you been back"? "I've been back a year now, Moses." "I was blown up from a huge blast not long after we started fighting". "It sure is good to sees ya". "And you too, Moses". Dale does manage a smile knowing his friends have made it through the war. "I came down to see the parade and maybe see some old friends."

It is a good day. Dale and Moses talk for some time catching up on the last few years.

"Moses I work right here at the Station selling tickets". "That is sure fine fors ya Dale".

"Good bye Dale" "Good bye Moses" these fellow Soldiers and friends part company they say good bye and it will be some time before they see each other again. The occasion for reuniting will be Bill's upcoming wedding day. It will take a full two weeks of travel and practice for the wedding. There will be much fellowship time coming up.

Bill reaches Camp Funston in Kansas only to find dismal, at best health care and facilities for recovery. One ray of hope comes walking in, this is Nurse Maybelle Johnson. Maybelle is a sixty five year old nurse who was summoned to help some of the soldiers on the frontier fighting Indians. This going back to just after the General Custer battle of the Little Big Horn.

"Hello!! Mr. Bush, great day to be alive!!! "Here, try this buffalo stew". "It will make you grow horns and stand right up"! "If you know what I mean". Bill was chilling from a fever and didn't say much but "thanks" when he could.

"I'm your nurse I will be here for you so you can whip this pneumonia". Maybelle was in charge of about twenty men in the hospital. "I will give you another bath later". Bill didn't realize she had given him a bath at all; he was sweating from the fever and out of his mind for a while. "Your sister and one brother were here to see you but have gone home now". "You were too sick to know they were here". "You also have a pile of medals over on that dresser". "You were out for that ceremony when the Generals come in".

"You don't happen to have a friend named Dale Bird do you Bill? "Yes, I do have". "He was here for some while". Maybelle gives Bill the bad news about Dale. "He is missing an arm and his face is disfigured on one side." "He is still a handsome man though."

Bill is happy to hear Dale has made it back even with the problems. "You were out of your head talking with the fever and said his name a few times". "You are very fortunate you don't have the influenza". "There have been many deaths over it and it is spreading across the whole country like a wild fire". "They don't want anyone spitting or coughing or sneezing without covering their mouth". There is a poster out in the hallway wait till you see that." "Up at Camp Devens they say 100 men and women are dying each day". "Someone said the Germans are behind this with germ warfare". "Who knows"?

You really get to know your nurse when you are down sick; all formalities are put aside so service can be provided. Many months go by and Bill has made a comeback.

"Thank you, Maybelle", Bill says, "you are truly heaven sent", all these months taking care of me and the boys here. "I believe the prayers and your buffalo stew did make me a new man". "Thank you. how can I ever repay you"? "You already have Bill" says Maybelle "by just being thankful". "I'm going home tomorrow and I'm long overdue". "We will all miss you Bill". Bill had found the strength to help Maybelle for about the last three or four weeks. Bill has been at recovery for eight months himself. "Good bye, Maybelle" "good bye Bill". Bill is packed and ready to travel. "Tell that Dale hello for me if you see him".

The steam clouds and monstrous shadow from the locomotive is cast on the small depot at Camp Funston named after "fighting Fred" Funston. Funston helped organize help for all the survivors of the big earthquake in San Francisco, California on April 18th 1906.

Fred had also written a book on large scale deployment of troops. He was the only man to lie in state at the Alamo. He had died just two months before America entered World War one. Fort Funston is modern day Fort Rely in the middle of the state of Kansas.

Bills return home route will take him back through the Union Station in Kansas City. This will only be for a whistle stop then on to Chillicothe, Missouri. Excitement builds inside Bill with every blow of the whistle and rocking motion of the train. He is as happy as he has been for quite a while. None of the north Missouri boys are coming home together but all are coming home. Bill is the last doughboy going home.

Bill falls sleep coming home and has another dream concerning a boy hood happening. He is all smiles as he remembers the day when he and Dale and Moses all get some tobacco. They all go out behind the barn and the three boys roll it tightly into cigars and smoke themselves sick. They all go home and are more sick. Poppa was unconcerned for any punishment and did think it funny as Bill remembers. This brings another smile thinking about home and Momma and Poppa and all his family.

HOME COMING

————•——

*B*ill has recovered from the pneumonia after some months and is now discharged from the Army. He has some money in his pocket from his service time and is on the train heading for home. It is a beautiful spring, Sunday morning when Bill steps off the train in Chillicothe Missouri. Bill has missed all the accolades, for the returning soldiers. No one is at the station because it is a Sunday morning and most everyone is at church. Bills own family is twenty miles West in the town of Breckenridge. Bill drops in on a church service, as he walks in with his uniform on he has some service medals on his chest for bravery and different campaign and battle bars, all the people turn their heads to see the rugged young man especially the young ladies. "Howdy" is all he can get out before the service starts.

As Bill leaves church he shakes hands with the Pastor, You have strong hands young man!! Then, one elegant, older woman tells Bill "We are having a church picnic later on this next month on the 15th". "You should plan to come back young man" "Thank you, I will". Some of the girls ask his name and make time with him for a short while.

Bill is on his way to see home for the first time in four years. Not much has changed in the rural community of Northern

Missouri that you can see. The wheat is still green in the fields. It is 1921 Bill is homeward bound. The Breckenridge community is half the size it was before Bill left for war.

Bill was offered a buggy ride half the way to home by a man from that Church he visited. "How was it over there fighting? The buggy driver is asking. The delayed response is "Well, it really wasn't pretty sometimes and it was a little muddy." "Thanks for the ride" sir." Bill will walk the rest of the way as Bill walks he pictures home in his mind he sees the breeze blowing through the wheat fields just like those ocean waves he just crossed over. Bill finds his Momma and his Poppa as if he had never been gone. "William!!! Poppa exclaims, all of the family is, as you might expect, overjoyed and surprised to see their brother and son. "So handsome you are" says Momma.

"Moses Johnson came by and told us you were sick and where you were". "He is doing fine but his brother Otis is still in Leavenworth prison". "Yes" "I'm going to go visit him when Moses goes".

"There is something you don't know Bill". "What is that Momma"? "Your friend, Dale Bird, Moses saw him in Kansas City". "He was wounded severely he lost an arm and is disfigured on one side of his face". "My loving nurse, Maybelle Johnson has told me".

"She was Dales nurse first". "Maybelle and Dale were talking during Dale's recovery and he was speaking to her about where he was from and some of his friends". "Praise and Thank God Dale made it back".

"I'm ready to get to work for now". Bill will make a return trip down to the city when the work is caught up.

"Thank you, Bill", Says Momma; "Poppa has been much slower these last few months". Poppa knows too that Bill needs to be a partner now of the farm. Farms are businesses that need constant attention. Bill is ambitious and a very hard worker. The next few weeks an enormous, amount of work is accomplished by Bill. He is really jumping into the work with his now older brothers and really Bill is showing some leadership skills as well. Bill is a serious man.

Time passes by quickly and that church picnic is on Bills mind "I'm going down to Chillicothe this next Sunday if anyone wants to go". The conversation at the Bush's dinner table has become brisk since Bill has come back. With much to catch up on and many exciting stories to hear from Bill. "Yes!! I will go" says Bill's Sister Suzette she is quite the good-looking young lady by now. Bill will never tell of the most exciting time of being in the Ark. It will never be brought up until he is old himself. Bill and Suzette are at the church picnic getting a cold drink, some of that new soda pop that is being served by Grace and some of her church, girlfriends. "Hello" and thank-you for the drink. "Yes sir" Grace says politely "you're welcome". "Are you new here"? Just visiting I'm here with my sister.

"We thought her your girlfriend" Grace says. "I don't have a Girlfriend". Were you in the War? Yes I was, I'm only back this last month at home in Breckenridge.

Breckenridge, "I've not been up that way much". "The German settlement isn't it"? "Yes but we are very much German Americans and have been for many years". That fact was never brought up again between them.

Well, "welcome home soldier" "we are happy to have you back and here at our church"! It is some time before Bill has a steady woman friend and even thinks to have a wife. He is involved with the farm and he is yet to settle down.

After a few visits back to that Church and talking with Grace a few times he and her do things together. They enjoy some ice skating that winter "Do you enjoy skating, Bill"? "Yes, I can give it a try anyway". Grace was always full of energy and liked being active. The two also enjoy some walks in the park. Grace's Sister Hazel is always with them as chaperone. "Well Hazel what do you think of this Bill Bush"? "Is he the one"? "I believe he loves the Lord and would make a find husband for you". "He is handsome too", the two giggle.

Finally one Sunday morning at church their "eyes meet" The next spring Bill gets up enough gumption to ask Grace to marry him. They are engaged to be married in one year.

Bill is off to Kansas City to visit Dale Bird. This visit is long overdue. He finds him working at Union Station as the Ticket Master. "I'm glad to have this job Bill". "Yes, we all need work". "I'm happy you made it back Dale". "I'm happy for you to Bill". "Are you married yet"? "I'm just engaged to Grace Whitacre of Chillicothe, she has a sister named Hazel". "I remember them both Dale says they were just kids that lived not far from us". "They lost their father to a fire". "Yes". Dale asks about Moses. "I haven't had much time to talk with him. I hope fine". "Dale I need to ask you a favor" "go ahead and ask" "will you be my "best man" at my wedding"? "Yes, I would proud to be your best man". The two reunited friends are happy and reminisce some about being at Union station before the war and old times as children.

"I will send you an invitation so you know all details and can travel up next year". Really only ten months from now. "Good luck" and "God Bless" The men shake hands and hug.

Bill has some time to think on the way back and is thinking how Dale still has a great attitude toward life and has accepted his situation. The New Testament Author, Paul writes "I have learned to be content in all circumstances."

Bill still has some unfinished business, the visit to see Otis. He will need to find his brother, Moses Johnson.

Moses is working delivering fertilizer as he had done before the war. He also has a job at the train docks unloading freight cars at night in Chillicothe.

There is a Thanksgiving holiday coming up, giving Moses a day or two off from working two jobs. This will be the opportunity to go visit his brother and Bill will go with him. It is a trip of about 160 miles west and down South some to Leavenworth prison. This prison was just completed by 1910 before the war had started. It is now 1922 and Otis has been in since 1916. "Hello Bill" Otis is very upbeat and joyful. "Moses"!! The brothers hold each other for the longest time and are brought to tears. It is a grand reunion. Three hours go by so fast. Otis says, "I believes I knows who raped the Girl".

"It really wasn't a rape at all she had done wrong with that boy from Brookfield". "She just said I had done this to cover up her wrongs". "Her dress was torn and stuff and she was found out by her mother". "They both made up the lie that landed me here". "I found this out much later from a friend who had overheard the boy bragging about what he had done".

"I only have four years to go Bill." "I can make it because my brother is back from the war and have a friend like you". "I can make it because I have the" Lord to help me". I can do all things with the Lord who strengthens me. Philippians 4:13 "I have started a Bible study in here and more are coming to the Lord all the time". "The Lord is good". Moses and Bill must leave; all give hugs, and now have more confidence that one day Otis will be free.

As Moses and Bill leave town they notice some men taking hard looks at Moses as a black man. The Ku- Klux- Klan has been making a comeback and is back stronger than ever. Moses and Bill hasten out of town to avoid trouble.

"Moses", "yes Bill" "we need to go visit that man over putting Otis in prison and that woman and her mother". "Yes we do Bill". "They should be ashamed of themselves".

Moses and Bill go and confront the mother and daughter. "You have taken a man's life away from him" Bill says to the mother. "You have taken a brother away from a family". "You are liars." "God hates a liar". "Get out", is the response. "We will, but God have mercy on your souls for this offence".

THE MOST BEAUTIFUL BRIDE

*B*efore Bill is married he makes a spiritual decision. As he had listened to the pastor since returning home. Bill was convicted in his heart to repent and went "forward'. He was baptized as a boy but now has more discernment as a grown man and goes forward to renew his faith and commitment to Jesus and asks to be baptized as a man. The next Sunday he is baptized and he is a great testimony to many people at church. Bill will be committed to the Lord for the rest of his life.

The month of April has finally arrived. The wedding date has been set for a year the preparations for this wedding have been great. This will be the biggest wedding ever in the town of Chillicothe, Missouri. The church is decorated with wonderful colored flowers all down each side. The women and girls are all in bright colored dresses and hats. The bride's maids are all have matching dresses in light purple. The men have on their Sunday best. Bill has a full suit and vest. "Dale" Bill shouts "you look great"! The best man is there with a woman friend, Rebecca is her name. "Glad to meet you Ma'am" Bill with that slow drawl. "What a day to get hitched" Dale says. "How is it in Kansas City"? You know on that hill across from Union Station? "They are going to build a monument to the Great

War there". Bill has got to the point of not hearing much and has really little on his mind but Grace.

It is time to gather the wedding party. The pastor has gone over instructions for both sides. "Do you have the ring" Pastor asks "Yes", Dale has it in his care." Pastor and Dale had met the night before at the wedding rehearsal. "Are you nervous Grace"? Asks Hazel, "not much but some I must admit".

Grace is in a long white wedding dress with very detailed, pattern in the fabric. She has a white lace veil on her head and a white corsage on her wrist. She is in her prime and is radiant. "How do I look"? "Wonderful, Beautiful"!!!! Hazel gives her the nod and smile for confidence.

The wedding starts with the usual procession of the Bride coming in last with a fill in Dad. Mr. Bird, who is still alive and comes up from Kansas City with Dale and is asked to give Grace away in her own father's absence. The guests are in place, the music begins, Bill, Moses and Dale, everyone is waiting for the Bride.

Grace appears on the arm of Mr. Bird. With her naturally curly hair and blue eyes, she is radiant, smiling, and a perfect bride for any good man to cherish for life.

"We are gathered here to unite this couple in Holy matrimony" "If anyone here has a reason that this couple should not be married please let them speak now or forever hold your peace". There is only silence. "Do you Grace Whitacre take this man William Bush to have and to hold in sickness and in health for better or for worse till death do you part?" With a great smile Grace responds "I do" Do you William Bush take this woman to be your lawfully wedded wife to have and to hold in sickness and in health for better and for worse till death do you part"? With another great smile Bill says "I do." "Do you have the ring"? "Yes" "Thanks Dale" This ring is a symbol of unending Love and bond. The ring has no end. "Please give the ring". "With the power vested in me I now pronounce you man and wife". Ladies and Gentlemen I present to you Mr. and Mrs. William Casper Bush. All are clapping for them. "You may kiss the bride." Yeah!!! There will be a reception for the couple downstairs and all are invited thank you. Many gifts were given for them.

"Well you did it congratulations", "Thanks Dale", "thanks Moses". Even Moses is dressed up with a suite and looks very handsome. Moses and his wife were already married as Moses had got back from the War. The couple even has one child and one on the way. They live outside of town on their farm.

After all the wedding crowd is gone and the couple says good bye to many friends.

Bill and Dale say goodbye, "well come down to visit in Kansas City when we can Dale". "Maybe you can return the favor of best man for me Bill". "Yes Dale you can count on it."

Bill had decided to take Grace to the Elm's hotel in Excelsior Springs, Missouri.

They have a hot springs to relax in there and it is a nice place. They will be gone for a whole week.

Grace and Bill would have lived through the remaining, 1920's the 30's the 40's and most of the 1950's before I had any memory of them.

Those decades would have prohibition, a stock market crash and depression era another World War and a Korean conflict. The world powers are just starting what they call the "cold wars" by the late fifty's'.

The couple persevered through these times of uncertainty, poverty, family troubles

and disappointments. I had never seen them argue or look unhappy. They were able to find us something to eat whenever my family would show up. I often wondered if my parents let them know in advance of our visits. I take away fond memories of seeing a perfectly kept garden by the now gardener Bill who won "best garden" awards. I always had a sweet tooth and I found that honeycomb honey was my friend. Grace was the "best cook" she gave "basic needs" that are cherished memories but I take away more, I take away modeled love, simple love, a commitment to love. A modeled partnership. The man is the man and the woman is the woman. No fighting over whom is in charge because they both know that the Lord Jesus Christ is Lord over all, owner of all who believe.

Another famous "Bush family" meeting is convened with the business topic of the farm itself and the number of people it can support. Poppa is not completely in charge of the meeting it is a cooperative or group of the boys and their families. Poppa speaks

"The first order of business is the farm and its future". "Now that Bill is back he is the eldest and would have first right's to have a place here". We all know the limits of the production and adjustments must be made."

Bill speaks, "I want you all to know that I do wish to continue on the farm with you". "I truly love it here but I have been thinking though that Grace and I will move on." "I will find work". "Moses said there is need down at the loading docks". "This will solve the problem for the farm for now". There is silence in the room for a minute. Bill speaks again "I will ask for some help to build a home in the city of Chillicothe." Bill has taken the pressure off the family farm by stepping aside for the good of all.

"Yes!!! Bill", everyone speaks up, "we will help you build that house." The mood is joyful and somber at the same time. Poppa is brought to tears and is proud of his son even more for being such a man to do this for the family. "Thank you Bill"

A family dinner is planned and the focus is now on the new house for Bill and Grace.

A three acre lot is purchased from that Army money along with lumber. Bill draws up a floor plan and shows it to Alton.

"Where are your closets"? "You don't have closets". "Thanks I did forget them". "Well, no harm done but we need more space to allow for them". The house is expanded on paper. The lot is level but the problem is that the budget doesn't allow for equipment to dig out the foundation and craw-space area. The home is staked out on the ground. "Grab a shovel" Grelton says, Bill knows what is up. Bill and Grelton begin the task of digging the required dirt out by hand!! "Poor people have poor ways." Yes "we" do have. Progress is slow but soon some starts to show. The brothers work steady on the digging not to wear out themselves or their hands too quickly. After four straight days of sixteen hours the job is done. A fine accomplishment. The extra dirt is used to bunker a root cellar entrance.

Stone is brought in from the Bush farm for the foundation. Bill wants red brick for the outside and orders it from Acme Brick co. located in Kansas. There is plenty of time because the house needs to be built.

Bill's brother in law Orville will be the lead carpenter for the job. A lot of hammers are swinging and the home shapes up fast.

No power tools are used just elbow grease and manpower. The inside walls will be plastered. There is a plaster man that is paid the only man that is paid on the entire job. His work is flawless and the interior looks great. There are arched doorways in the home that show great craftsmanship.

The day comes when the brick arrives it is exciting because this is the last project to complete." I hope you know what you are doing Grelton with that mortar mix," Bill has some slight worry in his voice.

Four months have come and gone since the start of the digging and a new house is up and ready for the finishing touches like Drapes for the windows Grace will make them by hand. Bill has some painting to do in and outside.

There will be no air conditioning for the home but power is available for lights so for the first time in Bill and Grace's life they will have lights and running water in their home.

Move in day comes and all are helping. Hazel all the Bush family and half the towns

population it seemed. The pastor is asked to come in and bless the home. A great picnic is arranged on the front lawn, what a day it was to celebrate with friends." Now, live a simple life, for the Lord" the pastor says, with a toast to the young couple, and Bill and Grace did just that and they were happy.

Bill and Grace's marriage licence showing their names, William Casper Bush and Elva Grace Whittacre DATED April 26th 1925

LIFE GOES ON

*M*oses and Bill "best friends" since children now veterans of the Great War and family men now take jobs as "warehouse men" as they were called. Their job description was loading and unloading freight on and off the rail cars and any trucks that were in and out of the docks at Chillicothe.

Bill and Moses would work side by side for the next five years. The work was hard, physical and tiring. Neither man was the type to worry about a position in the company or complain of condition or their wages.

Bill and Moses didn't know but the American labor union organization movement had started. In many different aspects of the work force car factories clothing factories workers have been slowly making ground to improve working conditions by organizing their respective group of workers they are called "unions." Unions had been influential in achieving improved work conditions and by 1938 the Fair Labor Standards Act establishes the first minimum wage and the forty-hour workweek. Companies were just not willing to freely allow organizing of the labor force. So union busting gangs of men were hired to bust heads to discourage and intimidate workers. This tactic of busting heads is where Bill and Moses's metal would be tested again. Having survived the Great War together Moses and Bill, the two together are a force to be reckoned with. Two men in dark suits and ties showed up after a work shift to speak to the dockworkers. They explained to the men that management would never voluntarily give wage increases or holiday pay or vacations. They explained how the union would organize and negotiate for these concessions. What these organizers wanted was a person they could contact later to further help set up meetings of the warehouse workers. Bill was selected by the group as their representative the spokesman. This position would prove to be the next change in Bills life.

Bill is now the spokesman for the group of workers and accepted the responsibility. Bill though there would be no real problem, he was wrong. Finally one night as Moses and Bill finished their evening shift. Three men, Union busters made a surprise visit. "We are here to discourage you from any more union activity" "How do you plan to do that"? Bill answered sharply. At That moment, these men pull out oak, axe handles and approach Moses and Bill. These union busting tough guys don't realize they have just met "even more tough" men that themselves. Moses is able to block and stop the first handle hit, he then grabs that man by the head and throws him off the four-foot high dock, on his back. Using the same axe handle Moses cracks the head of another man, he to, is thrown off the dock. Bill has no problem out flanking the last man and has him down in a headlock while Moses disarms the tough guy. With a big "thud" the last man is thrown off the dock and all of them leave with threats being made as they run for their black, Ford sedan. "We will be back."

Eventually the warehousemen do organize. Both Moses and Bill receive a modest, raise but union dues are now required.

Bill and Moses now become more famous as fighters and protectors.

A FAMILY MAN

*B*ill and Grace had built their own home with Bill's Army money that provided materials only. Hard work and family help would finish it. God would bless it.

The idea that God invented for a man a helper, a woman and for the family structure to be a man and a woman. Was the greatest idea God ever had.

Families are for the purpose of raising a new generation of people, having children. No one even said raising children was easy. Having children would become the next great heartbreak and challenge in Bill and Grace's life.

"Bill"!! "Yes Grace what is it"? "I believe I'm pregnant"!! "Yippee"!!! "You are"?? "Yes I believe so I have missed my period for two months now". "Let me hug you that is great!! Honey". "We need to make plans, fix up the extra bedroom and finish the baby furniture that we have not made yet". "Yes Bill please make the baby bed for our child". "Honey do you think you could make a chest of drawers too"?!!! Grace is excited and is planning ahead for the new arrival. Unfortunately, it will be a long road for the Bush family to have their first born. Grace will have three miscarriages before their first and only child is born. The couple is faithful though that God will give them a child and he does.

Many prayers were eventually answered in God's own time. How precious and loved is a baby daughter, when she arrives. Donna is loved and will grow up in a loving Christian home. There is a difference in a family and home when God is honored in the family. The difference starts with the Father and Mother and their devotion to God individually and collectively.

THE TROOPER

———·◆·———

*B*ill knows a lot of different people in Missouri and his name comes up as a candidate for the new Police force being organized in Missouri. Unfortunately Moses was not selected because he was a black man.

"I will be just fine Bill". The two men are just like brothers despite the obvious color or race difference. "You take that new job, they needs ya". Moses encourages Bill to go on with his blessing, to become a Trooper. This new police force is called the Highway Patrol.

It is April 1931, as you know by now, April is Bills month. Bill is approached with the opportunity to join up for this new Highway Patrol. Bill and Grace now have to seriously consider this new opportunity. The wages would be better. There is paid health care and a retirement system. This would make a huge difference in their future if Bill accepts the position. The job does come with risks, being a police office is dangerous. Because men use real force to rob banks and commit other crimes. Also, organized crime had started in the nineteen twenties. The first Trooper killed in the line of duty in 1933 would be Sergeant Ben Booth, killed by a bank robber.

After much praying, Bill would become a State Trooper, as they would be called. Five thousand men would apply and only fifty-five would be hired.

The State Troopers would be under the Governor's direction for special projects as when the President would visit the state. Otherwise the Troopers were policing the many miles of highways.

Bill's training would be given in Saint Louis Missouri. For the next nine weeks intensive training will be given. Law enforcement, Firearm training and defensive driving is some of the special training given there. The graduates of Troopers were divided into groups for different sections of the state. There was a Captain for each of twenty men. All the troopers were issued .38 Caliber, Smith and Wesson six shot Pistols. Blue uniforms were issued along with distinctive, flat rimed hats.

After training was completed and graduation ceremonies and celebrations were completed. The troopers went to work in their respective assigned areas of the state of Missouri.

A Ford, four door, 135 horsepower hardtop, was the standard automobile issued out. Not many today would remember the cherry top light that was on the center of a Trooper's car or the very large, torpedo spotlight. Traffic policing was the basic work assignment with criminal chasing as a sideline. Many a Trooper would be killed by bank robbers and many killed by car wrecks in the years to come.

Bill was eventually able to be transferred close to the northern Missouri area where he and Grace have built their home in Chillicothe

The Great depression had started with the collapse of the stock market on October 25th Nineteen Twenty-Nine It was called Black Friday. The Hard times called the "great depression" had started and people became desperate. There were no jobs available for men. Families were losing farms or their homes.

Bank robbers would become almost folk heroes. They were sometimes called champions of the people. It is hard to understand that thief's and killers could be looked up to all, but they were. The bad guys had even started using more firepower that the Troopers or police had issued to them. Some bad guys had automatic weapons.

Bill had sent home his own Thompson Sub Machine gun with plenty of ammunition. When he began his work he decided to have the gun available to him in the car under his car seat.

Now if you know anything about Bill by now, you know he is a fierce fighting man and calm and cool headed under fire. We could talk about being not afraid or fear. Bill was a believer of Jesus and the bible. Bill had great confidence and loved the Lord.

Matthew 10:28 Do not be afraid of those who kill the body but cannot not kill the soul. Rather be afraid of the One who can destroy both soul and body in Hell.

As life did go on as a Missouri State Trooper Bill would be put to the test in service. In the early nineteen thirties many bay guys were on the loose and many escaped from prison with help from the outside. Most all of these men were on the FBI most wanted list. The bad guys were called public enemies. Pictures of these public enemies were posted in all post offices in the United States and many other public locations. After reading about these men you find out that most started out as boys doing petty crimes then they keep going and meet other old criminals and then go on to much worse crimes.

One of these criminals was named Alvin Karpis. Alvin was a Kansas native. Alvin was doing time in Lansing state prison and escaped with the help of the Barker Gang. Alvin eventually would be a public enemy number one.

Bill was usually patrolling US 36 in North Missouri. This stretch of road runs East and West across America. If you go north from Lansing or Leavenworth Kansas about 50miles you would hit US 36 highway. That is exactly what Alvin Karpis was about to do.

St. Joe Missouri is on US 36 highway and is very near the Kansas and Missouri border. St Jo was the turnaround point for Bill and a rest stop. Just as Bill was approximately 10 miles from St. Joe traveling west when a car that was speeding whizzed past him. Bill made a quick turn around and made the pursuit. Bills car was faster and he caught up. Then an unexpected slam on of the brakes of the speeding car happened, causing both cars to slide sideways.

Alvin and the other man jump out firing their automatic weapons. Bill will think quickly and react keeping his calm and reaching for his own trusty Thompson, Bill rolls out the other side of his car under fire and returns fire. The bad guys are more than surprised. Alvin is not hit but the other man is. They retreat to their car and go. Bill fires as they leave and then finds his car full of bullet holes and the car has two flat tires.

Later it is found out that the one bad guy did die of his wounds. Alvin escapes. J. Edgar Hoover the head of the FBI would be in on the capture of Alvin a few years later.

"How was work honey"? Grace asked. Bill didn't wish to alarm her. "I had a flat tire, took some time to repair." Bill had received a flesh wound and kept the wound to himself not wanting to alarm Grace.

Grace found out later about the bullet holes. Many years go past with not as much action as that one night but there were the terrible auto accidents to deal with that were always very ugly.

By the time World War Two started for America on December 7th 1941 Bill's career was half over. 10 years later it would be over. There was a modest retirement party in the Chillicothe Trooper office. Bill was an exemplary Trooper and had received many awards. A very nice pocket watch was given to Bill and he signed his retirement papers.

All of this life Bill had lived before I was three years old. Retirement was calm for Bill with his garden and church life. I really did enjoy Bill's honeycomb, honey that he had from his own hives. When I was five or six years old I could start remembering honey and homemade biscuits and still do remember they were very yummy!!!

LAST CHAPTER

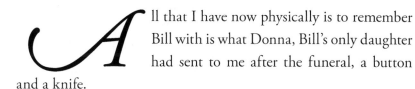

*A*ll that I have now physically is to remember Bill with is what Donna, Bill's only daughter had sent to me after the funeral, a button and a knife.

I wish to speak about Bills burial for a minute. It was modest with a good presiding Pastor. The elegy was a to the point message about how God takes care of some of his own for just a little longer than others on this earth. A person needs to think about how long life can be.

Terrie, my sister and I were present making the trip from Kansas City with my Uncle Bill and my two aunts Evelyn and Betty. Bill and Grace had out lived most of their friends so there weren't really other people there.

Imagine 100 - Christmas', 100 - 4th of July's to celebrate. Try living 60 and 80 year marriages, 40 and 50 year retirements. We all need to live life at the proper speed and remember where we are going, Heaven.

Jesus made a promise to go to the father and prepare the way for us. "For in my Father's house there are many Mansions" He then promises to come back and take us with him. *John 14: 1-4*

The button that I have is from a coat worn into battle and the knife has been sharpened 100's of times and used in Bill's garden and with the beehives he kept season after season.

A knife that also carved a likeness of what he seen a world away from Missouri and made from the teak, wood he found there.

Bill and Grace, just two people in one of those oval pictures, forgotten about now.

Old Bill a man when he was younger met Thomas Lawrence, Just missed shooting a then young Adolph Hitler. Shook hands with his commanding officer Dwight Eisenhower, and Douglas McArthur.

As I had told you our family visited Bill and Grace back in the fifty's later in the sixty's our family was broken up by my parents' divorce. I lost track of them for many years until I was grown and on my own.

It was many years later that my sisters Terrie and Kerrie and myself would make the trip to Tulsa, Oklahoma. The last visit we would have with Bill and Grace being together in life. We all enjoyed a good meal that day. Before leaving that evening, the sun was nearly set and it was near dark. We didn't turn on the lights in the kitchen so it was almost dark in the room, all of us stood in a circle, holding hands and prayed before leaving.

We never know our time it was only few months later that Grace went home to be with the Lord. When I get to heaven I want to see Grace, I want her to tell me again "David" always drink plenty of water it is good for you". That is good advice for a young boy.

They took Grace back to Chillicothe, Missouri for her burial.

Before Grace had past there was few months of suffering for Grace. Bill was even more the devoted husband and was her main care giver as she was in bed most of the time. He would read to her and give her water. Each day she would eat less and drink less. She would say "one day closer to Glory" as the days went by.

Another many years later when Bill was becoming a centurion, my entire family including Aunt Betty, Uncle Bill, my son Andy his family we all went to visit Bill. He is residing in a Tulsa nursing home by then.

I was so impressed with his living place in the Tulsa Nursing Home. It was like a small home but it was an apartment with his own private kitchen, bedroom, and a living room it was wonderful. Bill if he wished, had only to walk about 25 feet down a short hallway to a dinner table where he enjoyed the company of his friends, other residents at the home that could walk well. You need to understand that Bill was still helping the "old people" off the church bus when he was 86 years old himself.

This group of spry residents would sit at the dinner table and tell jokes, they were a riot.

One of the visits was to celebrate Great Uncle Bill's One-Hundredth birthday. We have many pictures and a movie recording of the event

The last visits were good ones Bill would tell of his bee keeping and his gardening.

"Clover honey" that is the best and sweetest kind he would say. I had heard these stories

many times but I never tired of them. Bill told of how he and other soldiers would be moved by train at night for the next day's engagement with the German forces.

Finally on our last visit with Bill we took my Father-in-law, Andrew Peknik who is a World War Two veteran. He fought in Europe just as Bill had done in WWI and with the army infantry too. This last visit is a good visit; we walk into the Tulsa nursing home looking for Bill's room. He has been moved now and he has a room 'buddy."

This was so funny, we went to the room looking for Bill and we can't find him.

I went to the center desk and asked the male nurse, where is Bill? This is a classic answer "Oh, he is out running around visiting more than likely." Later we found him in the bathroom.

I had neglected to tell one story about Great Uncle Bill. After Bill had retired and had his prize winning, garden he would sit on the back porch and crack nuts with a hammer. He became close friends with two squirrels and they would get lots of those nuts. One day one of the squirrels came up to the door and hit it as to tell Bill it was dinner time. Bill even fed them by hand and most of the time they would turn their back to Bill watching for danger knowing that their backs were safe with Bill there.

As I stood there in Bills room that last visit, I stared at the plaque on the wall next to Bills bed. This was the plaque given to him by the Veterans of Foreign Wars (VFW) in Chillicothe. He was the last surviving World War One, veteran from Chillicothe, Missouri.

Next to that plaque was a picture of Grace and Bill together. You know, their picture was in one of those oval picture frames.

The End

SUMMATION OF THOUGHTS
FOR THIS BOOK

———————

The fact that, friendships are vital to us and can endure through time.

The fact that a marriage any good marriage, can endure through time and life hardships if the pair is focused on God.

The fact that, families can endure through time and stay together.

The fact that, the glue for our relationships isn't just believe in God.

Rather it is putting our faith into practice, doing what the bible tells us to do.

Matthew 7:26, 27 "But everyone who hears my words of mine and does not put them into practice is like the foolish man who build his house on sand. The rain came down, the streams rose, and the winds blew and beat against that house, and it fell with a great crash"

The fact that, death is part of life and we never know our time.

Matthew 24:44, you also must be ready, because the Son of Man will come at an hour when you do not expect him.

The greatest commandment *Matthew22:37, 38, 39, 40 Love* the Lord your God with all your heart and with all your soul and with all your mind. This is the first and greatest commandment. And the second is like it: love your neighbor as yourself. All the Law and the Prophets hang on these two commandments.

LIST OF REFERENCES USED

Leavenworth military Library

The First World War / an eye witness history- Author / Joe H. Kirchberger

The Experience of WWI - Author / J.M. Winter

K.C. Star Paper 1-17-99 Article about Fighting, Fred Funston of Kansas

Leavenworth public library

A pictorial history of the United States Army / Gene Gurney

The Holy Bible / Men's Devotional / New International Version/ my personal copy

Letters about Bill and Grace / Donna and Olin Boyer daughter, son-in-law / Tulsa, Oklahoma

Union Station, Kansas City / Jeffery Spivak

Gun Digest 1970 edition / edited by John T. Amber

On line information, internet for inventions and events

National geographic map of Persia / Iran

Real life living experiences

Visits to the World War One memorial museum in Kansas City, Missouri

NOTES

Printed in the United States
By Bookmasters